COWBOYS
AND
ANGELS

Other titles by the author

Ticket to Ride
We're Gonna be Famous
Hatred is the Key
Too Big to Cry
Love Shack
More Than a Woman

COWBOYS
AND
ANGELS

Graham Sclater

To Trevor
Best wishes

Enjoy

14.9.2017

TABITHA BOOKS

Published in 2017 by Tabitha Books

Copyright © 2017 Graham Sclater

Cover design by Denise Bailey

ISBN 978-0-9954884-1-0

Typeset in 12pt Sabon

Front cover photo Andy Dean

Tabitha books is a division of Tabitha Publishing Limited

Exeter EX2 9DJ England

Tabithabooks@tabithamusic.com

www.tabithabooks.webs.com

Acknowledgements

Andy Dean for the cover photograph, Denise Sclater, Phil Ray, John Artes, Ray Kemp, JP & TC at Venture Radio, Steve Osborne and all the radio presenters and media around the world who continue to support me, and lastly all the readers who have bought my previous work.

Photo Barrie Cutler

Graham Sclater was born in Exeter and still lives in Devon where he is a successful music publisher and author.

Prior to returning to England in the late sixties, he was a professional musician in Germany and a session musician in the London studios where he worked with many name artists. Graham writes in many genres and his first novel *Ticket to Ride was* published in 2004 by Flame Books and republished by Tabitha Books in 2006. This was followed by the novella *We're Gonna Be Famous*; and the novels *Hatred is the Key, Too Big to Cry, Love Shack, More Than a Woman* and now *Cowboys and Angels*, which is Graham's seventh novel.

He is currently working on several television and film scripts as well as his next novel while he continues to build his music publishing company and record label. Graham can regularly be seen on cruise ships where he talks about creative writing.

Thanks to George Michael for his wonderful song and title of this novel.

'You owe me, Malik. There is nowhere on earth for you to hide and you will pay for what you did to me.'

Prologue

Harry Clark was about to turn off the radio in his timeworn Land Rover when the voice of the early morning local radio DJ attracted his attention. 'That was *Hazard* by Richard Marx, a very apt song for such a snowy morning.' He coughed. 'Take care all you drivers out there ...' He faded out the record and continued in an annoyingly cheery voice. 'A lot of thought goes into this show – we don't just throw it together,' he said, as he laughed into the microphone. 'Now, I've got a request for Harry Stryker Clark.'

Harry shuddered, sat bolt upright in his seat, and turned his head towards the radio. He craned his neck as he listened intently.

The DJ continued. 'Harry, or do they call you, Stryker?' He paused and laughed to himself. 'Is this for real?' He didn't hide the scepticism in his voice as he continued. 'Well, Harry, if you *are* listening on this cold snowy morning – whoever you are.' He paused. 'This is for you.' He nodded to his female producer and continued to laugh. 'Your lucky friends over in sunny Cyprus are wishing you a very happy birthday.'

As the music faded in, Harry exploded. 'It's not my birthday. It's not my birthday. I said ... IT'S NOT MY BIRTHDAY!'

CHAPTER ONE

Good Day Sunshine

Dawn was about to break. As the waves gently ebbed and flowed up and down the almost deserted beach, they dragged the pebbles and shingle back and forth creating a surreal whooshing and rattling sound.

An Arab dressed in flowing robes stood at the water's edge. He turned slowly and nodded to an unkempt man in jeans and t-shirt who was standing beside a rusty mini-bus parked awkwardly on the nearby beach road.

The man twitched nervously and nodded back to the robed man.

As he looked out across the Mediterranean, the Arab shielded his eyes from the piercing rays of the sun as it rose above the horizon. He watched the fishing boat slowly heading out to sea and, when it was little more than a speck on the skyline, he pulled a mobile phone from his ankle length robe and flicked at the pre-programmed number.

The expansive Mediterranean bay was calm, deserted, and silent except for the buzz of the lone motorboat as it made its way towards the bustling port. A tanned Harry Clark sat back and slipped a cigarette into the side of his mouth. He took his time to light it while he continued to steer the second-hand Sea Mark 23, a seven-metre converted fishing boat, with one hand. Harry was thankful to have had the small boat while he carried out the initial works to the roof of the building of what would be his future home and bar. The tiny cabin at the front had been invaluable when, for the first few months, Harry had slept in it while he collected recycled materials from up and down the coast.

The fish quay was bustling and noisy as the locals ambled from stall to stall, laughing and cackling to each other. The instantly recognisable tourists, enthused by the infectious sounds of Greek music, were aggressively cajoled by the vendors.

Harry Clark, a well-built man, in his mid-forties, heavily freckled, with fine sun bleached medium length hair, wore a creased grey t-shirt, a well-worn black leather waistcoat and faded denim jeans. Clearly excited by the noise and activity, he pulled alongside the quay and leapt ashore. He tied up his boat and made his way between the stalls acknowledging some of the local people and fishermen with a smile or a nod and the occasional shaking of hands as he walked.

When he reached the old town he strolled into the local supermarket. It was early in the morning and almost empty except for a handful of tourists wearing the obligatory shorts and flip flops, something he would never wear. He walked instinctively between the aisles until he reached the newspaper stand. He scanned the front pages and finally settled for the Cyprus Mail, the Greek daily newspaper, a copy of the locally printed Daily Mail and a free copy of the monthly magazine the Paphos Times. He walked up to the till, paid for the papers, shared pleasantries with the cashier, and left. Keen to read the latest news he stopped at his favourite Greek Cypriot taverna, sat at a table overlooking the harbour and ordered a coffee. He knew he wouldn't be disturbed except for the occasional good morning from the regulars. He spent the next hour contentedly skimming through each of the papers. He then folded them neatly and, after paying for his coffee, slipped them under his arm and left.

Harry walked slowly through the market, dodging the sudden surge of tourists, and stopped periodically by his preferred stalls, closely examining the fresh fish, fruit, and vegetables, before checking the list given to him by his chef, Mama. Harry double-checked his list to make sure he had everything on it. Overloaded with his purchases Harry made his way through the market towards his boat. He jumped onto the boat and a man, who had been sitting under a dirty white tarpaulin, passed him the food and newspapers, untied the boat, and threw Harry the rope.

Harry thanked him in Greek, and the local man replied with a toothless grin.

After carefully stowing everything on the boat, he started the engine and with a final wave to his willing helper he pulled away.

Ben Lake, a young English student, ambled along the quayside. He noticed the flag; the large red "H" and the words "Harry's Bar" beneath it on a grey background, flapping out across the water at the end of the breakwater. He walked along the breakwater and sat at an outside table facing the harbour.

Harry's Bar had a large shaded terrace which ran much

of the length of the breakwater. At the end was the two storey building constructed of the locally sourced ashlar stone. The building housed the bar, a large kitchen, four bedrooms, shower and bathroom, as well as a storeroom which doubled as Harry's workshop. Hidden within the storeroom wall were two fireproof safe compartments with security locks to which only Harry knew the codes.

Ben, in his early twenties, wearing a white long-sleeved shirt, stonewashed chinos and deck shoes, looked out of place with his pale complexion amongst the sun-tanned tourists and olive skinned locals who were enjoying the early morning sun. He flicked at his long dark brown tousled hair and, having had too much of the sun, moved to a table beneath the sprawling grapevines. He shook his thoughts away when a pretty young waitress, her dark hair tied in a high ponytail, walked out of the bar. She initially ignored Ben and methodically placed freshly ironed grey and red check tablecloths on the empty tables, securing them with metal clips before placing a menu beneath the decorative glass bottles of olive oil.

As soon as she finished she walked across to Ben. 'Good morning.' She forced a smile. 'Welcome to Harry's Bar. Can I help you?'

He chose not to make eye contact with her, instead he raised his head slightly and tried to hide his blushes.

She continued. 'We aren't serving food at the moment.'

He spoke softly. 'That's fine ... just coffee.'

Ben stretched down and reached for a book from his leather shoulder bag which he'd already hung on the back of the chair. Taking his time to clear his throat, he swallowed hard. 'Please.'

She returned after a few minutes carrying a tray, placed his coffee on the table and a glass of water beside it.

He mumbled his thanks without looking at her.

'Would you like anything else?' she asked.

Ben placed his book, unopened, onto the table and raised his head. He forced a smile. 'No thanks,' he said.

She fluttered her long eyelashes, which immediately drew Ben's attention to her beautiful dark brown eyes. She returned his smile and skipped off towards the kitchen, flicking her fingers in the hot tub as she passed and wiping them in her red apron.

As he sipped at his coffee Ben heard the sound of Greek music playing across the breakwater. He put down his cup and looked around for the speakers.

He failed.

Harry had taken his time to conceal the speakers and cable amongst the overhanging vines that had woven their way through the bamboo panels, which in turn gave welcome respite from the hot sun.

Harry had noticed the war-ravaged building when he had visited Paphos twenty years earlier with his then new wife, Xanthi. Back then, not even in his wildest dreams, did he think he would eventually be able to lease it.

The nineteenth century fortification was built by the British at the end of the wide breakwater to protect that part of the vulnerable coast from possible invaders. It had remained in a dilapidated condition since 1955 when it was bombed by the Greek Cypriot militant group, the National Organisation of Cypriot Fighters (EOKA), and left in disrepair as a reminder of those violent times. The lengthy breakwater leading to the building was protected on one side by a two-foot-thick stone wall, which at more than ten feet high towered above it.

When Harry was pensioned off from the forces as a result of his horrific injuries, he returned to Paphos to convalesce. When he saw that the building had remained in its dilapidated condition, with large holes in the roof and many of the windows blown out, he knew he had a reason to get well. He took a twenty-five-year lease on the building and was granted permission to convert it into a restaurant and living accommodation. There was one proviso, Harry couldn't put up any signs on the building. He soon came up with a plan to get over that obstacle – the flag.

He wanted to renovate the building externally to resemble its original condition. He took his time to search out sympathetic and original recycled materials from dealers across the Greek Cypriot sector of the island as far as the security zone at Nicosia, annexed by Turkey in 1974.

When Harry finally started to plan the design and layout of the bar he knew that in the summer, the hottest months of the year, it would be too hot to sit directly in the sun. He knew tourists and locals alike would welcome the cooling sea breeze at the end of the breakwater. The addition of the unique hot tub, tucked in the right-hand corner near the entrance to the bar and shaded by the bamboo and grapevines, was cool and would be fought over by visitors during the hottest time of the day. Whilst at night they would enjoy the warmer water and feel pampered with drinks served directly to them.

Mama, the chef, a very large Greek Cypriot woman responsible for all the food at Harry's Bar, was busy in the kitchen chopping tomatoes, onions and garlic. She sang along to the music playing out across the terrace and jigged while she worked.

Nyla entered and danced with her. 'He's nice,' she said, excitedly.

Mama inched back the edge of the curtain, peered onto the terrace and looked across at Ben. 'Um,' she said, thoughtfully. She smiled at Nyla and grinned. 'They're all nice when they're that age.' She dug Nyla in the ribs. 'Then they get fat and lazy,' she said, with a loud lewd laugh.

Nyla pulled away. 'Mama, you're terrible,' she shrieked before walking off in disgust.

As the fishing boat made its way slowly along the island, the Turkish captain was becoming more and more irritated by the muffled moans and cries from below deck. He shouted angrily at his crewman. 'Keep them quiet down there,' he screamed.

Reluctantly, the crewman left the bridge and slammed the door behind him. He walked across the deck and opened a small hatch near the bow.

The shaft of blinding light cut through the darkness to reveal emaciated men, women and children. They shielded their eyes as they looked expectantly towards the light.

The foul stench hit the crewman full on and he pulled his head back in disgust. He pointed his gun at the human cargo and waved it randomly around as he climbed inside the hold and slid down two steps. 'Shut it up! You wanted this. Don't give me any more shit ...' He glared at each of the adults in turn. 'Or, I'll kill yer.' As he scowled at them they pulled back in terror. He continued as his eyes darted from one to the other. 'And ... not another sound.'

He cocked the gun. 'Remember what I said.' He snarled. 'Quiet!'

Their faces looked back at him in abject terror and they all nodded subserviently.

Overcome with the stench, he covered his mouth. 'Good,' he added, speaking through his clenched fingers. Gagging, as he made his way back to the deck, the crewman slammed the hatch closed and threw the bolt, returning the pitiful cargo to its hellish world of darkness.

CHAPTER TWO

Born To Run

A group of dark skinned Arabic men wearing western clothes sat around a makeshift table in the dilapidated warehouse. The shafts of light that permeated the holes in the corrugated metal roof illuminated the crates and boxes and the table littered with empty bottles, open tins and plates of unfinished food. They all smoked Arabic cigarettes and the thick acrid smoke was exaggerated as it flowed across the warehouse, highlighted periodically by the rays of light. They all stared attentively at a large wipe board and Malik, a middle aged Iraqi man dressed in an expensive hand-made suit, as he drew feverishly on the board. 'To make this work we have to be quick,' he said.

He paused and took his time to scrutinise each of them in turn.

The largest of them was Bear; thick set, solid and a little under six foot tall with a long bushy beard. Akram, a well built, shaven headed man, who stood proud and erect at well over six foot tall. Ghalib was much shorter than any of them and, having trained in martial arts in Asia, was Malik's preferred bodyguard; not that Malik felt he ever needed one.

Malik's driver, Raheem, was the only one of his henchmen that wore a suit. His long hair was raked back tightly from his forehead and tied into a ponytail exposing the numerous tattoos on his neck.

Yusuf, a tall, thin, black skinned man, in his thirties, stood at the entrance well away from the rest of them. Although he listened to Malik's instructions, he was preoccupied with ensuring their security was not compromised.

The sixth of his henchmen was Gassiev, the only non-Arab member of Malik's crew. Gassiev, a misfit from St Petersburg, was a few inches over six feet tall, with high cheek bones and epicanthic folds which narrowed his eyes, and a snubbed twisted nose which had been broken in combat with an ISIS fighter. He was a loner and preferred to be well away from everyone else, remaining in the shadows and watching events from a distance. Malik met him when he was fighting in Afghanistan then, when the Russians pulled out of the country, Gassiev deserted and left for Iraq where he and Malik continued to fight together as mercenaries.

Malik continued. 'I expect you all to do exactly what I've told you to do.' He looked at them for confirmation. 'Is that clear?' He brought his hands down hard on the makeshift table. 'I said, is that *clear*?!'

While all the Arabs nodded simultaneously, Gassiev chose to rock his head, stretch his neck and cross his arms.

Malik continued. 'No mistakes. Okay?' He rose from his seat and straightened the jacket of his silk suit. 'Then let's go. And remember ...' He clenched his fists and raised them into the air. 'No mistakes.'

They stood up and moved hastily towards the exit in silence.

Yusuf remained in the warehouse while four of them walked

past the car and towards the wharf where they climbed into a brightly coloured speedboat. Akram took his place in the driver's seat, fired up the powerful engine, and raced out of the dock leaving heavy swell crashing onto the wharf.

Raheem opened the rear door of the Mercedes and waited patiently beside it.

Malik stood on the wharf and watched the speedboat power away from the quay and allowed himself a self-congratulatory grin before climbing into the rear seat of the Mercedes. Raheem gently closed the door behind him before getting in the front of the car and pulling smoothly away.

Harry turned out of the harbour into the open sea and made his way along the coast. He slowed down and shook his head as two jet skiers raced wildly across the bay. He muttered to himself. 'Crazy bastards.'

His mobile rang loudly but he was unable to find it. He cursed as he bent down and searched amongst the bags of food until he eventually found it beneath the large bag of mushrooms. 'Yeah – hello.'

The jet skiers continued to race blindly in the direction of the fishing boat.

Harry looked up from his telephone as the boat came into his eyeline and bore down on the jet skiers.

They still remained totally oblivious to it.

He could see what was about to happen and his face exuded total shock.

The jet skiers crashed into each other and as the ship powered over them they disappeared beneath the deepest part of the sea around Cyprus.

'What the … ?' He focused on what he had just seen. 'I'll

call you back,' he said. Harry slid his mobile into his waistcoat pocket, turned the boat and raced towards the area where the jet skiers had disappeared.

The fishing boat continued on its journey.

Harry reached the spot where they had fallen but could only see one of them in the sea. He reached out to the long haired man and dragged him to the side of the boat. 'Are you alright?'

He choked his reply. 'Fine.' He spat out a mouthful of water and continued. 'Yeah, I'm fine.'

'Hold tight and stay where you are,' ordered Harry.

Harry ripped off his waistcoat and t-shirt and kicked off his navy canvas beach shoes. He took a deep breath and jumped into the clear Mediterranean. He dived down into the sea and continued until he saw the man, still on the jet ski, struggling to free himself from the mass of old fishing nets. Harry powered himself back towards the surface and burst out of the sea.

'Your mate's trapped. Just stay there,' he ordered.

The long haired man nodded his head wildly in agreement.

Harry took a huge breath, dived much deeper and swam towards the now unconscious jet skier. He flicked open the brown leather pouch on his belt and pulled out his Swiss Champ army knife. He effortlessly cut through the old nets that had ensnared him and after a few anxious and desperate moments he grabbed at the man's legs and freed them. The jet ski sank slowly to the sea floor still entangled in some of the weed enveloped nets.

Harry grabbed the unconscious man around the waist and raced towards the surface. He hauled him into his boat and began to administer CPR.

The long haired man, still in shock, hung on to the side of the boat and looked on anxiously. 'Is he gonna make it?'

Harry sucked in air and continued with the CPR. He took a deep breath and, with a concerned look, he spoke. 'He's got a chance.' He continued with mouth to mouth resuscitation and continued to massage the young man's chest until his patient vomited. He reached into a box beneath one of the seats and pulled out an old blanket that he kept for the occasional cold evening. He wrapped it tightly around the trembling man.

Harry could be seen to physically relax and he smiled at the other young man still in the water. 'He's gonna be fine,' he said. He reached out and without any effort hauled the shivering jet skier onto his boat. He took an old woollen jumper from a canvas bag and threw it at the long-haired man. 'Put that on,' he ordered.

Harry continued to look at the men while he pulled a worn woollen jumper over his own head. With his arms still outside the jumper, he spoke. 'What the hell were the two of you thinking ... racing about like idiots?' He shook his head to partially dry his wet hair and slid his arms through the sleeves. 'I was in two minds whether to leave you both there.'

The long-haired man pulled a face. 'Would you have done that?'

Harry continued. 'It's what you both deserved.' He threw back his head and sighed. 'Why is it that you people?' He sighed. 'Think you can do what you like when you're over here?'

'I know,' said the man apologetically. He reached out to shake Harry's hand. 'You saved our lives – so you ought to know who we are. Right?'

25

Harry shrugged. 'Really? Do you honestly think I need to know that?'

The long haired man ignored Harry's remark and continued. 'Anyway, I'm Jamie.' Harry slowly shook his head from side to side to signify his indifference and waited expectantly. Jamie continued. 'Me and Ryan are ...' He coughed and cleared his throat by spitting over the side of the boat. 'Well, we're on holiday. You know what it's like ...' He smiled shamelessly. 'Sun, booze and ...' He stopped suddenly. 'But why didn't they stop to help?'

'Who?'

Jamie pointed at the diminishing outline of the fishing boat heading away from them. 'Surely they saw us?'

Harry shrugged. 'No idea,' he said. He threw his head back and shook the remaining water out of his hair. 'Who cares?' He took his time to study each of them and continued. 'Just let me get the two of you off my boat and I can get on with my day.' He checked on Ryan and tucked the blanket tightly into his body. 'Um ...'

The colour slowly returned to Ryan's cheeks and his breathing was now almost back to normal.

Harry turned to Jamie and pointed at Ryan. 'He'll be fine.' He smiled broadly. 'I hope you've got the money to pay for those jet skis.' He sniggered. 'They don't come cheap.' He smiled to himself while he waited for their reply. 'I can tell you.' He paused. 'Ten thousand euros each,' he said slowly.

He steered towards the shore and accelerated away.

CHAPTER THREE

Turn Back Time

Ben sat at the table preoccupied as he took photos of the harbour on his mobile phone and emailed them to his parents in England. Nyla walked towards him with a brightly coloured, laminated menu. 'Are you having br ... ?' She was interrupted by the deafening sound of the high revving speedboat and turned towards it. The brightly coloured boat roared up alongside the bar and three men jumped onto the breakwater.

They made a grab for Nyla.

As she fought back, she kicked out at the tables and chairs, knocking them across the breakwater.

Mama watched from the kitchen window and tried desperately to scream.

Silence.

Ben looked on open-mouthed as they seized the now screaming Nyla.

In a well-executed manoeuvre, the kidnappers covered her head with a black bag, dragged her towards the speedboat, and threw her into it.

Ghalib raised his hands threateningly and screamed at Ben in broken English. 'Don't move. OK?'

Akram finished his sentence from the helm of the speed-boat. 'And don't call to anybody. Eh?'

Ben's face lost all colour as he frantically nodded his reply.

'Let's go!' yelled Akram. He gunned the throttle and they powered off causing a massive swell which spewed over the breakwater and reached some of the chairs and tables nearest to the edge.

Malik sat at a table outside a taverna on the quayside. He clicked his manicured finger nails on the table and took huge drags on his cigar as he watched the speedboat roar away. He smiled to himself, finished his coffee, and walked slowly towards the Mercedes and Raheem, his waiting driver.

Police cars, some of whose blue lights continued to flash, were parked haphazardly on the breakwater as close to Harry's Bar as they could without moving the tables. A helicopter buzzed overhead and the police photographers flashed enthusiastically as they took pictures of the scene. The whole area was a hive of activity. The uniformed policeman, Inspector Andreas Zavos, resplendent in a peaked cap, emphasising his position of authority, waved his arms excitedly as he directed the police who were milling around recklessly looking for clues.

Ben was stunned and shook his head erratically as he tried to make sense of what had just unfolded in front of him.

Mama sat at a table on the terrace and trembled. She bawled her eyes out as she rocked back and forth in her chair.

Satisfied with his achievements in directing his officers,

Zavos marched across to the hysterical Mama. He stood directly in front of her, spread his legs apart and crossed his arms. 'If you can't give me any information how do you expect me to help?' He looked down at her and frowned.

She shook and wailed uncontrollably.

The Inspector reached out and patted her hands before continuing in a much softer tone. 'The longer you take – the worse it will be for ...' Without warning, he suddenly lost his patience and slammed his fist on the table. 'Come on – they might kill her!'

Mama broke down and mumbled incoherent drivel.

Zavos shook his head and signalled to the only policewoman to comfort Mama before he walked across to Ben.

He spoke to Ben in Greek.

Ben replied by shaking his head uncontrollably and opening his arms and flapping them around in mid-air.

The Inspector continued in English. 'Can you do better than her?' he asked, pointing at Mama. He adjusted his cap with his black leather, gloved hand.

Ben looked blankly ahead and mumbled his response.

Zavos continued. 'I said.' He coughed loudly and spat the phlegm into the sea. He wiped his mouth with the back of his glove. 'Can you tell me something?' He straightened his whole body and stood to attention before he continued. 'Anything?' While he waited for a reply he leaned forward and drilled his fingers repetitively on Ben's table.

There was only silence and a further shaking of Ben's head.

Zavos persevered but this time he spoke in a subdued, desperate rasping voice. 'Anything?'

Harry pulled up against the quay, threw the rope to the nearest policeman who tied up his boat, and jumped out. He crossed his arms as he looked around at the chaotic scene. He shook his head in disbelief before finally shouting at the Inspector. 'Zavos, what the hell is going on?' He didn't wait for a reply, instead he rushed towards Mama, yelling at her in Greek as he ran. 'Mama, can you tell me what the fuck is going on?'

Mama tried to speak but continued to blubber uncontrollably as she tried to speak. She gabbled her reply. 'It happened so quickly, they came ... grabbed her ... and ... and ... they left –'

'Grabbed who?' raged Harry.

'Nn ... nn ... nnn ... Nyl ...,' mumbled Mama.

Harry rushed across to the Inspector, stopping a few inches from him. 'Zavos, surely you can make some sense of this?' he said, pointing randomly around at the chaos.

Zavos took his time to light a cigarette. He took several huge drags and exhaled foul smelling smoke before he replied. 'Not yet,' he said, nonchalantly. He adjusted his mirrored sunglasses and looked across the harbour before turning to look directly at Harry. 'Why would they take the girl, eh?' He took another drag and carefully studied the glowing tobacco before replying in a slow matter of fact manner. 'I mean, she's young. She's pretty –'

'Don't even go there, *Zavos*,' roared Harry.

The Inspector pulled back and smiled through his heavily nicotine stained teeth. 'OK, Harry,' he said, with a snort. He reached out to give Harry a reassuring tap on the shoulder.

Harry pulled back.

'Come on Harry, you must relax. We'll find them,' he said. And, as if to emphasise his concern, he took his time to remove his sunglasses and look directly at Harry.

Harry glared back at him.

Zavos faked a cough and took his time to replace his sunglasses. He straightened them before signalling to his officers to return to their cars. They fired up their engines, the blue lights flashed and the high pitched wail of the sirens resumed as they reversed along the breakwater.

Zavos moved as close to Harry as he dared before whispering into his right ear. 'We can't do anything else here, Harry.' He pulled on his right glove. 'I'll keep you informed of any developments.' He moved towards his police car, opened the door, and as he leaned on it he looked at the upturned tables and chairs before returning to face Harry. 'And if *you* hear anything.' He lowered his voice. 'Please let me know. I'm sure you understand ... this is police business. Don't think you can deal with this one yourself,' he said, emphasising the last word. He finished his cigarette and flicked it into the sea. 'It may be personal – but leave it to us, OK?'

Harry stood motionless and exhaled erratically.

Zavos waited, indicating his impatience by tilting his head slightly to one side until Harry grunted his agreement. The Inspector closed his door and with a wave of his hand indicated to his driver to leave.

Harry shook his head in disbelief as he watched the last police car leave. He stood alone on the deserted quay and took his time to try and take in what had happened, and why. A fierce and determined expression spread slowly across his chiselled face. He picked up the overturned tables and chairs and repositioned them before walking into the bar. As he walked, he dragged his hair back through his open fingers. He pulled out a chair and sat at the table with Ben and Mama.

Mama pushed back her chair and nervously crossed the bar,

taking care not to make a sound and break the ghastly silence. She made three coffees and placed them gently on the table.

It was clear no one knew what to say and didn't want to be the first to speak.

They sipped at their coffee in silence.

Harry looked Ben up and down and finally spoke to him. 'Who the hell are you? What are you doing here?' Before Ben could answer Harry continued. 'You saw what happened, right? Can't you remember … anything? There must be something?' He tried to maintain his coolness but the tone of his voice was becoming harsher. He stood up and looked out of the window before turning back and returning to the table. He glared at Ben and the anger in his eyes cut right through him.

Ben fidgeted nervously in his chair.

Harry continued. 'Come on. Surely *you* can remember something?'

Ben pushed himself into his chair and the legs grated on the floor.

'What about their boat?' asked Harry. 'What colour was it? Did it have a name?' He smacked his forehead with frustration. 'A number – anything?'

An idiotic smile crossed Ben's face. 'Well … I took a photo,' he said, quietly. He pulled his mobile phone from his pocket and held it preciously in his hand.

Harry reached across the table and tried to grab it. 'What? Show me! Why didn't you tell me before?' His fingers twitched with a combination of anger and anticipation. 'Come on – show me,' he demanded.

Ben pulled back, clearly not wanting to give up his only link to the outside world. 'I dunno,' he said, anxiously.

Harry shot him a reassuring smile.

It worked.

Ben wiped his finger across the phone screen and passed it to Harry.

Harry stared at the blurred photograph for a few moments before looking up and smiling for the first time. 'I don't recognise it.' He studied it more closely. 'But there can't be too many like that around the island.' He referred to it again. 'That's some beast.'

Ben nodded as he remembered the noise of the powerful engine. 'Yeah,' he murmured.

Harry seemed more hopeful and walked towards the door. He turned and looked at Ben. 'Come on.'

Ben remained in his seat and mouthed to Harry. 'Me?'

Harry nodded his reply before stabbing his finger at Ben. 'Yeah. You.'

Ben took his time to stand up and, after glancing nervously at Mama, he reluctantly followed him.

Harry waved his mobile at Mama and spoke in Greek. 'If you hear anything ... you be sure to call me.'

She nodded enthusiastically and wiped at her eyes before forcing a smile.

When the speedboat carrying Nyla approached the run-down industrial area, Bear threw the rope to Yusuf, who caught it with his huge hands and tied it up. The kidnappers jumped out and bundled their hostage onto the quay before marching her into the warehouse. With her head still covered, they pushed Nyla onto a chair and tied her hands behind her back.

Ghalib and Akram stood nearby and drank beer while

Bear sat down at a makeshift table and simulated reading the Greek newspaper.

Nyla moaned and kicked out.

Gassiev reached across and tore the bag from her head.

She glared at him and growled as she shook her head, expressing her indifference.

Bear looked up from his paper and shouted at her. 'Cut et out,' he said, in broken English. 'If you give us any problim … we will have some fun.' He let out an obscene and vulgar laugh before he continued. 'Then kell ya, eh?' He clicked his tongue noisily highlighting his repugnance. He continued to laugh and licked his lips as he looked around at his accomplices and imagined the depraved and vile pleasure he had in mind. They all turned, eyed Nyla lecherously, and made revolting gestures before breaking into loud odious laughter.

CHAPTER FOUR

Everybody Hurts

Harry made his way slowly towards the harbour and, while he mentally checked out everything that moved around him, Ben sat in silence, too frightened to speak.

Ben finally cleared his throat with a nervous cough. 'That waitress was pretty... but what's the big deal?' He shook his head. 'I mean ... the police will find her.' He paused. 'Won't they?'

Harry was preoccupied and didn't hear him.

Ben continued. 'Why do we have to chase around? Do you look after all your staff like this?'

'Staff?!' screamed Harry.

Ben flinched.

'She's my daughter!'

'Wh ... ?'

Harry glared at Ben. 'Is that reason enough?'

Ben blushed and blinked his reply.

Harry eyed Ben and realising he had terrified his passenger, he smiled to himself. 'OK.' He paused and spoke in a low voice. 'Look, if it's any consolation … I'd do it anyway. I'm not having scum get the better of me.'

He offered Ben a cigarette.

Ben shook his head.

Harry lit his, and after a few drags appeared more relaxed.

Ben gulped for air and stuttered with embarrassment. 'I'm sorry – I didn't realise.'

Harry looked at the young man and, for the first time, realised that he was probably the same age as Nyla. 'Why would you?' Harry pulled his head back and took a closer look at him. 'The thing is …' He appeared too embarrassed to continue as he flicked the cigarette skilfully between his fingers. He sighed before raising his head and looking at Ben. 'I only found her last week,' he said softly, trying to hide his embarrassment.

'You found *your* daughter … last *week*?' Ben was obviously very confused. 'How come?'

Harry reminisced. 'I met my wife in Limassol back in the 90's … when I was serving here in the army.' He sniggered. 'We got married … and …'

Ben looked on expectantly.

Harry took a long drag on his cigarette before he continued. 'And, Nyla was the result.' He nodded and forced a proud smile. 'We were both too young and after she was born … we split.' He couldn't hide his regret. 'I had my career … I wanted it so bad.' He nodded his head thoughtfully before he continued with a shrug of his shoulders. 'Just wanted to fight …' He gave Ben the widest of grins. 'So that was that.' His mood suddenly changed and he wrung his hands. 'Then …'

He turned away from Ben and gazed out to sea. He continued. 'Three years ago the bastards pensioned me off.' He couldn't control his anger and gripped the boat's wheel as though he wanted to choke it. He finally acknowledged Ben's considerate face and grinned. 'So I came back to the island and took a lease on what was a once beautiful, but wrecked, building.' He looked back across the bay. 'I took years doing it up.'

'Why so long?'

'It was all my own work and I used materials as close to the original as I could.' He smiled proudly. 'I know every inch of that place so if there are any problems I can fix them myself and not use what is the local excuse for *tradesmen*.' He grinned. 'And when I opened last week who should turn up and ask me for a job?' Ben nodded. 'That's right. Nyla,' he said, 'I had no idea. It was only when I got a call from Xanthi, her mother, I knew who she was.' He let out a heavy sigh before he continued. 'So, now you know.'

Ben looked on, speechless.

Harry revved the engine hard and as he accelerated away he threw Ben onto the deck, where he landed in a heap. He shouted above the engine. 'Just keep looking, eh?'

The Mercedes pulled up in front of the dilapidated warehouse. Raheem leapt out and opened the rear door. Malik ignored him and, holding his mobile tight to his ear, walked into the warehouse. He straightened his jacket with a tug of the other hand. He nodded animatedly to the caller and closed his mobile. He glared at Bear. 'How are we doing?'

Bear said, 'She threatened me with her father.' He laughed loudly. 'Whoever he is?'

Malik strode towards Nyla and slapped her across the face. 'Superman is he? Eh?'

Nyla spat at him and then grinned brazenly at him. 'Is that the best you can do?'

Malik raised his hand again but thought better of it and sneered at her. 'We'll be long gone before anyone finds you.'

Harry tied up his boat at the bustling quayside. He pointed at Ben's mobile phone. 'Go and get that picture printed.'

Ben jumped off the boat and stood on the quay. He looked back at Harry. 'How many?'

'Get as many as you can?'

'What?'

'I'll pay. Don't worry about the money. Just do it.' Harry shouted after him. 'And put *your* mobile number on them.'

Ben looked back at him with a quizzical look. 'Mine?'

'Just do it,' screamed Harry.

While Ben walked off towards the shops, Harry moved slowly amongst the floating pontoons in the harbour and methodically checked every boat.

Ben and Harry walked along the fish quay, moving between the crowded market stalls handing out copies of the photograph to the local stallholders. As they pushed their way amongst the tourists and locals they took care to show everyone the photograph of the speedboat.

Each time, they were met with the shaking of heads.

An exhausted Ben and a frustrated Harry sat in silence on his moored boat in the harbour, deep in their own thoughts. As they sipped at their takeaway coffee, they were oblivious to the movement as other boats came and left the harbour. Harry subconsciously fingered the remaining photographs with his free hand and without warning blurted out. 'Look we've got two left so let's think about this.'

Ben jumped to attention and found it difficult to maintain his balance.

Harry steadied him and he sat back down. 'They wouldn't be stupid enough to leave something like that on public view after what they've done.'

Ben didn't react.

Harry stared hard at Ben and waited.

There was no response.

Harry drummed his fingers on the side of the boat and waited. When he finally had his attention, he continued. 'Would they?'

Ben didn't respond.

Harry took his time to study Ben. 'So what *were* you doing at my place?'

'I was a student at Birmingham University but took a year out to travel.'

'What are you studying?'

'Horology –'

'What the fuck.' He shook his head wildly. 'Is that ever going to be of any use to you?'

'You never know, do you?' replied Ben defensively.

'I think, I do,' said Harry. He flicked his cigarette butt into the sea. 'It's shite.' Harry lit another cigarette and conceded with a wry smile. 'OK. You may be right.' He shrugged. 'We all need to know about time – right?' He sniggered to himself. 'So where have you been so far?'

Ben blushed. 'This is my first stop.'

'Really?' said Harry. He laughed so raucously that Ben's face reddened with embarrassment. Harry took his time to catch his breath and continued. 'So … where are you staying?'

'The Agapinor Hotel ... in the centre of the old town –'

'How can a student afford a bloody hotel?' asked Harry. He paused and sniggered. 'I suppose Daddy's paying –'

'He's a do –'

'A doctor, eh?'

'No, my father is a dog trainer.' Ben snapped at him and continued. 'For the blind ...' He glared back at Harry. 'And, it's *not* a hotel – it's a hostel – and really cheap,' he said, emphasising the last word.

Harry was taken aback at Ben's change in attitude.

Ben smiled and continued with a new-found confidence. 'And, *I'm* paying for it.' He cleared his throat. 'I'm going to Turkey next ... and who knows after that.' He grinned at Harry. 'But after the last few hours.' He reflected on the morning. 'I'm not too sure about anything anymore.'

'Why not hang around Paphos?'

'Maybe ... I will.'

Harry ignored Ben's reply. He pulled out the mobile from his waistcoat and dialled. 'Zavos, have you heard anything?'

Zavos replied in a slow deliberated and uninterested tone of voice. 'Strangely my friend, we have not heard anything. Not a word.' He paused and took several drags of his cigarette. 'No sightings and no demands at all.'

He waited for Harry's response.

There was none.

Harry could hear Zavos breathing heavily.

'Where are you, Harry?' asked Zavos.

'I'm behaving myself,' said Harry, reluctantly. He continued with a snarl. 'For the minute anyway ...' He swallowed hard. 'But if I find those bastards first,' he growled menacingly. 'The services of you and your men won't be necessary.'

'Be careful, Harry,' cautioned Zavos. Harry could hear the desperation in the inspector's voice. Zavos continued with a snigger. 'Even you're not above the law, my friend.'

Harry shrugged, closed his phone and slid it back into his waistcoat pocket. 'Come on, Ben. Where would you hide something like that?'

Ben tugged at his ear. 'It has to be on the water, right?'

Harry shook his head in despair at Ben's obvious answer. He checked his GPS and painstakingly followed the coastline with his finger until he heard the buzz of the approaching jet skis.

Ryan and Jamie raced up to Harry's boat.

'Haven't you two learnt your lesson yet?' teased Harry.

'You know what they say?' laughed Jamie. 'Get back on and do it again.'

Harry shook his head in disgust. 'Is that right?'

Ryan frowned to Harry. 'What's up with you, mate? You look so bloody miserable?'

Ben blurted out the answer. 'Harry's daughter's been kidnapped. By the men …' He showed them the photograph and continued. 'On this boat –'

'Really?' asked Ryan, looking concerned.

Harry managed to force a smile. 'It's a long shot. But if you see it – call me.' He crossed out Ben's number on the back of the photograph, wrote his mobile number, and handed it to Jamie.

Jamie slid it inside his wetsuit.

As they jetted away they both shouted back to him. 'We'll have a look,' they said, excitedly.

Harry shook his head as the swell from the jet skis rocked the boat. 'Madmen … total fucking nutters.'

CHAPTER FIVE

I Want To Break Free

Ryan and Jamie made their way slowly along the coast and turned into the run-down industrial area, taking in the towering cranes, containers, ships and barges. They were ready to give up until they saw the speedboat moored to the side of a large dilapidated warehouse. They stopped and checked the photograph. Jamie pulled out his mobile and dialled Harry's number. 'We've found it, Harry,' he said excitedly. He looked around. 'We're in the industrial area, near the containers and ...' He twisted his head around and took in his surroundings. '... A grain silo.'

Harry replied excitedly. 'I know it. Stay where you are.' He paused. 'And keep out of the way.'

While they waited, the fishing boat glided towards the quayside and tied up behind the speedboat.

'Isn't that the boat that ran us down?' asked Ryan.

'It bloody well is. The bastards that nearly killed us,' cursed Jamie.

They watched as the crewman menacingly herded the small group of emaciated people off the ship and onto the quayside.

They were handed over to the kidnappers who screwed up their faces at the stench, before shepherding them towards the warehouse.

Gassiev jabbed his gun into the back of the older immigrant. 'Quick as you can,' he threatened, in Pidgin English.

'Yeah, come on. Get a move on – hurry up,' screamed Ghalib.

The now terrified trafficked men, women, teenagers and younger children, followed by a sobbing mother clasping her baby tight to her chest, were herded towards the warehouse entrance. As they shuffled inside they were all made to stand against the wall beneath a rusty colonnade. When they noticed Nyla tied to a chair they stood and looked on nervously wondering what their fate might be.

Malik tossed a briefcase towards the captain.

He caught it with both hands, laid it on a pallet, and opened it. As he counted the money, the captain constantly switched his attention between Malik and his crewman. He trembled as he took his time to count it.

Much to the annoyance of Malik he then began to painstakingly recheck it.

The captain finally closed the case and reached out to shake Malik's hand. 'Good doing business with you,' he said, with a deep husky voice.

Malik chose to ignore his outstretched hand and wrinkled his nose in disgust.

The captain huffed and forced a smile. 'Until the next time,' he said, as he nodded and walked towards the door with his crewman.

Before they could reach the door, Malik pulled out a gun, tightened the silencer, aimed at them, and squeezed the trigger several times. He shot the Captain and his crewman in the back. He motioned to Ghalib to pass him the briefcase and as he laid it beside him he turned to Bear and roared. 'Now get those greasy bastards out of my sight.' He kicked at an empty beer can and missed. His body stiffened in anger. 'And take that rust bucket out to sea.' He let out a throaty guttural laugh. 'They'll probably blow it out of the water for us.'

Bear nodded and grabbed at their nearest legs and single-handedly dragged the two bodies towards the fishing boat.

Malik turned his attention to the trafficked people and sneered. 'And ... give them something to eat.'

Akram picked up the plates of half-eaten food and part finished tins from the makeshift table, dropped them on the floor and kicked them towards the starving people. They scrambled around pushing and shoving each other as they fought for the smallest of scraps.

After watching them scuffle, Malik sniggered and motioned to Akram to give them the part finished drinks. Akram grinned broadly and threw the bottles of beer and water into the air.

The bottles smashed in front of them.

Their reaction was a combination of disgust and disbelief as the much anticipated and precious liquid, mixed with shards of glass, spread across the dusty floor and soaked into the concrete.

Harry killed his engine and stopped a short distance away from the warehouse. He acknowledged Ryan and Jamie with a nod. He whispered to Ben and passed him his mobile. 'Get a picture of the boat. Make sure you include the silo and send it to Zavos.'

Ben took the photographs and immediately sent them. When he looked up Harry had already disappeared.

Harry took Ryan's jet ski and glided in silence to within a few metres of the warehouse. He leapt onto the wharf and made for the huge building. He took his time as he weaved in and out of the shade and bright sunshine at the rear of the warehouse.

He checked the doors.

They were locked.

He climbed effortlessly onto a low-level roof and tried the windows. He moved stealthily across the roof until he discovered a cracked pane of glass. He took his knife from the pouch on his belt and slowly worked the flaking putty until the glass came away with a sharp click.

A little boy turned and looked up keeping his eyes trained on the window.

Nyla noticed him and took care not to be seen as she also glanced up at the window.

Harry put his finger to his mouth and signalled to them to ignore him.

Malik continued to mumble into his mobile, unaware of what was happening outside.

Harry carefully opened the window and was part way through it when he felt a gun pushed hard into his neck. 'Get up,' growled Gassiev.

Unnoticed, Harry slid the knife into his waistcoat pocket.

Moments later Harry walked apprehensively into the warehouse, followed by Gassiev who continued to thrust his gun hard into his back.

Harry could already smell the immigrants' fear but it took

a while for his eyes to adjust between the bright sunlight and deep shadows.

Malik slipped his mobile into his jacket pocket and exuded an enormous smile. 'Well, well.' He lifted his left hand and faked a cough into it. 'Hello, Harry.' He turned to his hired help and waited until he had their full and undivided attention. He continued with a loud snort. 'Or would you prefer I called you ...' He paused and chuckled before he continued. '*Stryker?*'

Harry looked uncomfortable until his embarrassment turned to anger. He shrugged his shoulders and made a futile attempt to avoid the gun pressing into his back. Gassiev snarled and jabbed it harder.

'It's been a long time,' said Malik, as he tilted his head and scratched it before continuing. 'Four years?'

'Five,' replied Harry, dismissively.

Nyla looked totally dejected and tried to control a sob.

Malik motioned to Gassiev to pick up the rusty chain.

He obliged.

He wrapped it tightly around Harry's left ankle before winding it several times around the steel stanchion and securing it with a padlock.

Harry thrust his head in the direction of Gassiev and spoke to Malik. 'Why him?' He turned and stabbed his finger towards Gassiev. 'The Russian?'

'There's still a lot of Russian money on this island and I need to be able to keep an eye on it.' He smirked. 'I'm part of *their* inner circle.'

'You don't miss a trick do you, Malik?'

Malik shook his head and grinned demonically.

*   *   *

It was pitch black. Stryker, his face heavily smeared with camouflage paint and wearing Arab robes, looked through his night glasses and peered out into the darkness from his bunker overlooking the valuable Mosul Dam at Lake Dahuk. Nadhir al-Ansari, an engineer involved in the building of the dam, said, "If damaged, the floodwaters would take four hours to reach Mosul, and forty-five-hours to reach Baghdad. And more than a million people would be killed if a 'good evacuation plan' was not in place."

There still wasn't one.

So the dam had to be protected at all costs.

Stryker was one of only a handful of Special Forces still in Iraq at the request of their Government to "train" their forces.

A loud gunshot rang out and reverberated around the tiny bunker. Stryker's body lurched forward and he lay wounded. Malik, dressed in Arab robes and holding a smoking AK7, approached him. He looked down at Stryker and kicked out at him. Harry grabbed his leg and they wrestled for their lives in the confined space.

Another burst of heavy gunfire rang out and Stryker's body flipped into the air like a rag doll before slumping to the ground.

Malik pushed himself up, straightened his back, and kicked out once more at Stryker's lifeless body. He grunted his satisfaction as he left the bunker and walked into the dark night accompanied by the Shadow that had fired the deadly round. The Shadow turned, pulled the pin, and threw a hand grenade into the bunker before vanishing into the night.

Harry shook his head as he tried to erase the memory of those horrific events and his appalling injuries. He took his time to take in his enforced surroundings. It was evident that the warehouse had been closed for many years and though much of the equipment and machinery had remained it was now rusting and useless. The shafts of bright summer sunlight streamed through the holes in the rusting roof sheets, creating bizarre shadows, accentuated by the decommissioned conveyor belts that wended their way between huge gantries high above their heads.

Harry already had a plan. He clicked his tongue and grinned at Malik before breaking into a thunderous laugh.

Malik tilted his head in bewilderment and looked at him enquiringly.

Harry's manner suddenly changed and as he spoke he extended every word. 'But … I got *through* it.'

Malik ignored him. 'So, tell me, Harry.' His top lip curled and he grinned before it gave way to a cruel sadistic smirk. 'How are you?'

Harry didn't reply.

'I've been watching you work on that wreck of a building, like a beaver –'

'What?'

'Come on, Harry.' He cackled mindlessly. 'This is a small island.' As he thought, he ran his manicured fingers through his greying collar length hair. 'Well, this part of it is.' He grinned. 'So, come on.' He sniggered. 'Tell me the truth, my friend. How are you?'

Harry raised his head and stared bizarrely at Malik. 'Don't pretend to …' He wrinkled his nose in disgust. He sucked in air and expelled it through the words as he spoke. '… To care.'

Malik ignored Harry's reply. 'You know.' He bit on his bottom lip. 'I never thought you'd come back from that.' He drawled. 'You must be a hard bastard.'

Harry closed his eyes and reflected on what Malik had said. 'Maybe ... but you underestimate us. We look after our own.' Without opening his eyes he forced a defiant smile. 'I was evacuated by Chinook before being flown out in a Hercules, and treated in the operating theatre on the plane during the flight back to base.' His whole body rocked. 'It saved my life.' He cleared his throat. 'It was almost a year before I could stand on my own.' He gritted his teeth and as he slowly opened his eyes he waited until they seared right through Malik. 'And another year before I could walk.' He cursed. 'Do you know I was in a fucking wheelchair?'

'Willpower?' asked Malik, nodding thoughtfully.

'Anger!' roared Harry.

'A man after my own heart,' mocked Malik, as he fiddled with the gun. 'We're the same you and me –'

'We're not,' growled Harry.

Malik drew out each word and spoke slowly. 'Are you sure, Harry?'

'Yeah.' Harry nodded his head wildly. 'I'm sure. We live in very different worlds, Malik.'

Malik locked eyes with Harry. 'Do we?' he asked.

Harry narrowed his eyes to help him to focus through the arcing shafts of sunlight. He shook his head and grinned.

Malik continued in a droning, monotonous voice. 'Harry, did you ever have any remorse following orders from your ...' He paused, smirked at him, and then continued. 'Your, erm, Tony Blair.' He coughed. 'After what happened to you?'

Harry grinned. 'I wasn't trained to retire.' He paused. 'Anyway, it was you. You did it – not Blair,' he said, shaking his head.

Malik thought to himself. 'Do you know what, Harry?' His eyes drilled into him. 'You British should have left in 2003. But no ...' He lowered his head and shook it in disbelief. 'Blair wanted you to stay.' He grunted. 'Why? Uh?'

'I didn't make those decisions,' snapped Harry. '*We* followed orders.'

Malik grunted.

'Do you know what Malik? I dreamed of finding you again ... and ...' Harry snorted. 'You were a nightmare that just wouldn't stop.' He laughed to himself. 'And all the time you've been here ...' As he looked around he shook his head and grinned. 'Right under my bloody nose.'

Malik took his time to flex his muscles before he raised his shoulders and let them drop. He looked around at his men. 'Um ...' He forced a self-congratulatory grin. 'Come on, Harry, or should I still call you ...' He paused and sniggered. '... Stryker?' He deliberately extended each letter. 'You know nobody lives forever.' He sniggered. '*You* more than any of us should know that. You've done your share of killing ... Right?' He grinned and spoke slowly. 'Why did you do it?'

Harry screamed back at him. 'Because I could!'

Malik laughed loudly and briefly fell silent. 'So why?' he asked, softly.

Harry threw back his head and shrugged. He glared at Malik and made sure he cleared his throat before offering his response. 'It's what Stryker was trained for.' He sniggered as he locked eyes with Malik. 'To rid the world of evil double crossing bastards ...' He snarled and pointed at him. 'Like you.'

Harry looked across at Nyla and lowered his eyes. He continued. 'Maybe I have done my share of killing ... but not innocent men, women and children.' He took his time and studied the faces of the pathetic immigrants as they shuffled and tried to hide – to find solace in the shadows – while they fought off the flies that had followed their stench into the warehouse. Harry looked directly into Malik's eyes. 'Erm ... So now you're a people trafficker?' He cleared his throat with a stifled cough. 'I mean ... just look at those poor bastards.' He twisted his head towards the immigrants. 'What do you have in mind for them – after already robbing them blind?' He grimaced and lowered his voice. 'You'll murder them, right?'

While Malik took his time to visually check over each of them he rubbed his gun lovingly against his cheek. His whole face lit up. 'They're the lucky ones.' He shrugged. 'Um ...'

Following nudges from the limited English speakers amongst them, they all looked towards Malik and forced pathetic smiles.

'They will work,' said Malik slowly.

The illegals muttered to each other.

Malik pointed his gun threateningly in their direction and they immediately cowered and recoiled into the yawning shadows.

'Work? Doing what?' gulped Harry.

Malik took his time to point his gun at each of them in turn before his unyielding face gave way to a mischievous grin. 'I don't care,' he said softly.

Desperation and fear collectively crossed their faces.

'As long as I make money, Harry. Who gives a damn?'

Harry grunted.

'So, what's next Malik? Kill me and the girl too?' Harry taunted him. 'See who it hurts the most, eh?' He sniggered and continued. 'You've had enough chances to do that.'

He grinned crassly. 'You're pathetic. And each time, you've failed ...' He screwed up his face in disgust. 'Miserably,' he said, patronisingly.

Malik raised his hands above his head, stamped his right foot on the crazed concrete floor, and struck out at Harry. 'Enough!'

Harry dropped onto one knee.

The immigrants murmured fearfully to each other.

The little boy seized the opportunity and, unnoticed, crawled deep into the shadows and hid behind Nyla. He held his breath while he waited. When he realised he hadn't been seen, he fiddled blindly with the rope that tied her wrists.

Malik lowered his voice and grinned. 'What's happened to you, Stryker? You've resigned yourself to running ...' He chuckled to himself. 'Running ... a fucking bar?' He looked down at Harry and sneered. 'Come on, is that all you're capable of these days?' He laughed loudly. 'A fucking *barman*?'

Harry looked up at him. 'I had a second chance, Malik, and I took it.'

Malik grunted and fingered the gun.

Harry continued while he pushed himself up. 'So why me, Malik? What did I do to make you hate me so much?'

Malik glared back at him. 'You were in our country under falsehoods. *Weapons of Mass Destruction?*' He raged. 'Hah.' He carefully targeted a beer bottle and this time kicked out, sending it high into the air before smashing against the wall. 'Those murderous bastards – *Blair and Bush.*'

Harry swallowed in agreement.

'Because *you* and the Americans trained us,' said Malik. He stroked his chin. 'What makes you think we would suddenly become your fucking servants – your *puppets*?' He spat at Harry and took a huge breath before licking at his dry lips. 'Right?'

Harry inhaled deeply.

Malik continued. 'Would *you* have suddenly become submissive to *your* aggressors?'

He waited open mouthed but Harry failed to reply.

Malik continued. 'No. Of course you wouldn't.' He sucked in air and swallowed hard. 'You would have bided your time and done the same to me, yeah?'

'Maybe,' said Harry. He partially closed his eyes and took his time to focus on Malik. 'So, who shot me? Who called in the "wet work," Malik?' He took his time and turned his head towards each of Malik's henchmen. They stood firm and there was no indication that any of them was the attacker. *Was one of them, the Shadow?*

Harry scrutinised Malik's eyes to see if there was a glimmer of a clue.

There wasn't.

Harry said, 'I didn't have a chance –'

'Why should you have?' asked Malik. He grinned, showing his lone gold tooth for the first time. 'I bet there was a whole bunch of people in Iraq waiting for a chance to take you down, Stryker.'

Before Harry could reply, Malik struck him with the butt of his gun.

Harry fell awkwardly and lay prostrate on the floor. He wiped the blood from his nose and mouth with the back of his hand. He took his time to push himself up onto one knee and, without drawing any attention to what he was doing, he tugged at the chain with the hand behind his back, checking the tension.

'Fine,' said Harry. He paused. 'But why the girl?' he asked. 'What's she got to do with it?'

Malik grinned inanely and turned to his men who copied him. 'Stryker was smart, but Harry hasn't worked that out?'

Harry grunted.

Malik continued. 'We needed a diversion to get that lazy bastard Zavos and his buffoons out of his office and off the scent of our cargo.' He turned up his nose and let out an enormous belly laugh. 'It worked, "a treat" as you would say.' He stuck out his chest proudly and revelled in the moment. As he scratched at his chin his manner changed. 'I mean, I couldn't rely totally on the boy racers to get your attention could I?'

'Them?'

'Of course, Harry. Come on – money talks. Always has.' He faked a roar of laughter and tapped his foot on the brief-case of money. 'Always will. What I didn't expect was for that Turkish imbecile to run over them.'

Everyone looked towards the door as it grated noisily on the rusty rollers, flooding the entrance with bright light.

CHAPTER SIX

Big Boys Don't Cry

Bear walked in behind Ben, Ryan and Jamie and took his time to prod each of them with his gun. Their ashen faces emitted absolute fear as they lurched awkwardly into the warehouse.

Malik shook his head and danced mindlessly on the spot, performing theatrically to his captive audience. 'My ... my ... Harry.' He looked at the latest detainees and tutted. 'What a pathetic excuse for back-up.' He snarled. 'Has it really got so difficult to find someone – anyone – to work with you, Stryker?' He stroked his gun. 'This time ... it really is good-bye. 'And ...' He grimaced and produced a vile grin, screwing up his pockmarked face. 'I'll do it myself.'

The little boy released Nyla's hands and crawled back unnoticed into the shadows.

Nyla seized the moment. As she kicked out at the makeshift table she yelled out, 'STRYKER!'

Harry had seen the boy go to help Nyla and was waiting for the signal. He had already removed his knife from his pocket, opened it, and then hid it in his clasped right hand. As the table collapsed Malik lost his concentration and dropped the gun. He quickly regained his composure, crossed his arms, and stood defiantly while he waited for Harry to be overcome.

Bear and Yusuf rushed towards him.

Ben stretched out his foot. Bear tripped and fell to the ground. He regained his footing in a split second but it gave Harry time to prepare for their attack. They were no match for Harry's electrifying speed, accuracy and determination fuelled by his anger. Although his movement was restricted he grabbed at the now shortened chain and used it to flay out at Yusuf with one hand. The chain snapped Yusuf's ulna as soon as it wrapped around his wrist. Harry now turned his attention to Bear. He had already opened the corkscrew in his knife and eased it between his fingers. He slashed out and twisted it, ripping a huge chunk of skin and flesh from Bear's left cheek. The Arab fell back in horror, clasping his hands against his cheek. It had little effect and the blood pumped from the gaping wound, between his fingers, and dripped from his beard. Harry jabbed out once more and punctured his lung with the knife. Akram crept up behind Harry, grabbed his head, and held him in a face bar. Harry dropped his knife as his head was forced back. He appeared to submit but then suddenly threw out his chest and roared before biting several of Akram's fingers through to the bone. In excruciating pain, Akram released his grip and stumbled backwards. Now Raheem made his move but Harry had already straightened his fingers and thrust a spear hand strike deep into his rib cage breaking several ribs. Before Raheem could bend over, Harry head-butted him, slapped the side of his head with the flat of his hand, and burst his ear drum. Ghalib rushed forward, postured, and posed in various pseudo martial arts moves but Harry, using his free leg, spun around and caught him with a roundhouse kick, sending him across the warehouse and knocking Akram back to the floor.

Gassiev was the last man standing. He stretched his body and stood tall. He grinned as he walked menacingly towards Harry.

Malik snarled at him and he stopped in his tracks. He waved him back and forced a wry smile. 'OK, Harry.' His face acquired a hideous transformation. 'It's you and me,' he bellowed like a man possessed.

Without any warning, Harry pivoted on his chained left foot and struck Malik hard in the solar plexus with the side of his right foot. He followed up with solid chops to both sides of his neck and a fist in the centre of his face. He broke Malik's nose and he gasped for breath as he staggered across the warehouse to retrieve his gun.

Harry moved towards him but restricted by the chain strained in vain.

Without warning Malik's body stiffened, it rose into the air and froze. Then, as if in slow motion, his face drained of all signs of life. Blood oozed from the side of his mouth and his dilated pupils looked blindly through Harry. 'You bastard,' he slurred.

Unnoticed, Ryan had picked up Harry's knife and now twisted it in Malik's back before he released it. 'I owed you one … didn't I, Harry?' he gushed breathlessly.

Harry fired him a look of sheer fury. 'Who the fuck *are* you?' He raged. 'You robbed me!' He shook his head in disbelief. 'Do you have any idea how long I've dreamed of doing that?' he said, feeling every word as he exhaled and shook his head dejectedly.

Ryan passed Harry's knife back to him and, without

cleaning it, he slipped it into the leather case on his belt.

Before Harry had time to catch his breath the high-pitched sound of police sirens could be heard wailing in the distance.

'Ben, get me a photo of each of them.'

Ben looked at Harry open-mouthed.

'Go on.' Harry pointed to Malik. 'Him.' He paused. 'And the rest – just do it.'

While Ben reluctantly took several pictures of each of them on his mobile, Harry spoke to Malik's men in Arabic. 'Get that bastard's body out of here.'

Raheem grabbed Malik's gun, turned, ran to the Mercedes, and raced off, firing gravel and dust into the air in his wake.

Malik's remaining men looked at each other and hesitated.

'Go on!' screamed Harry.

Gassiev stood defiantly and glared at Harry.

Harry spoke a few words of Russian and Gassiev immediately moved to help the others. Harry screamed, 'Get the bastard out of here and ...' He paused before speaking vehemently and extending every word. 'If it was one of you that tried to kill me ...' He took his time to stare at each of them and spoke slowly, accentuating every word. 'I ... will ... find ... you.' He grabbed the bloody chain and swung it threateningly. 'Now get the fuck out of here.'

Akram, Bear, and Yusuf looked nervously at him and grappled with the dead weight of their leader. They man-handled Malik to the motor launch and fired up the powerful engine.

Harry screamed out in Russian as Gassiev walked calculatingly towards him. Harry knew what he was thinking. He shortened the chain by grabbing a handful of it and holding it tightly behind his back. The Russian reached into his pocket, took the padlock key and flicked it towards Harry.

It fell a few inches out of Harry's reach.

Gassiev pulled a defiant face.

Harry maintained eye contact with the Russian as he twisted his body and stretched out his right leg.

He couldn't reach it.

Gassiev smirked at him.

Harry released the retained section of the chain from his hand and with the additional few inches he was able to draw the key towards him with his right toe. As he picked it up he gave Gassiev a huge grin.

The Russian walked slowly towards the open door before breaking into a run.

Ryan looked at Harry and stuttered. 'Why did you let them leave?'

'Why do you think?' retorted Harry. 'If they found that bastard's body you would have had to explain his death. You're a murderer now – right?'

There was no reply.

'Right?' screamed Harry.

Silence.

He glared at Ryan. 'Agreed?'

Ryan lowered his head and nodded.

Harry passed the briefcase to Ben and told him to distribute the money between the immigrants. Ben flicked open the briefcase and passed handfuls of euros to everyone including the children. They reached out, grabbed the cash, and stuffed the notes into every pocket.

As the sound of the sirens and barking dogs reverberated around the dock, Zavos, flanked by more than a dozen fully armed policemen, rushed in.

Nyla embraced Harry and squeezed him tightly. 'You came for me. I didn't think –'

'You're safe now.' He stroked her long hair. 'Did you think I'd let anything happen to my little girl?' he said softly.

She didn't reply, instead she closed her eyes and sighed with relief.

Harry looked across at the Inspector and grinned. 'You're a bit late, Zavos. We showed you where we were.' He released his grasp on Nyla and raised his arms high in the air. 'What more did you want me to do?'

Zavos removed his mirrored sunglasses and let his eyes adjust to the darkness. He shot Harry an uncompromising look before he answered. 'Um ... OK, Harry. What happened?'

'They got away,' grunted Harry.

Zavos nodded thoughtfully. 'Okay. So they got away.' He grinned at him in disbelief. 'How many?'

'Four,' said Harry. He sniffed. 'Maybe five?'

Harry looked to everyone for confirmation.

They all raised their shoulders and shrugged.

Zavos didn't hide his frustration. He looked at each of them in turn. 'So none of you can tell me?' He raised his open palms. 'Nothing, eh?'

They all grinned mindlessly back at him.

Harry pointed towards the trafficked men, women and children. 'Don't be too hard on those poor bastards.' He looked at Zavos. 'It's not their fault they chose those vile animals to help them.' He sighed. 'I could easily have made that mistake myself five years ago.'

Zavos pushed on his sunglasses and straightened his cap. 'It is out of my hands, Harry. Achim Kallidis, my colleague at the Aliens and Immigration Unit Corner, will take care of things now.'

Nyla tugged at Harry's arm. 'Can't we help some of them?'

'We'll see,' said Harry.

As he guided her towards the exit she looked back at the desperate group and shouted to the two young girls. 'I will help you.'

They didn't believe her.

Harry's bar was festooned with coloured lights and packed with happy customers who sat drinking at the tables inside and out. Greek music filled the air, completing the party atmosphere. Harry and Nyla stood behind the bar while Ryan and Jamie, Ben, journalist, Nichole Mouzie and ex-pats Patricia and Julian Stephens and Jane and Ray Scott who sat on bar stools on the other side.

Mama and two young assistants walked out of the kitchen with huge trays of food. One tray was stacked with sea food; squid, octopus, red-mullet and sea bass laid on a bed of salad. The second tray was a massive tray of assorted meat; "lountza" – smoked pork loin, charcoal grilled lamb, "souvlaki" – pork and chicken cooked over charcoal, and "sheftalia" – minced meat wrapped in mesentery. The third tray was piled high with vegetables, courgettes, green peppers. okra, green beans, artichokes and carrots.

Everyone showed their appreciation with whoops, cheers and loud clapping. Harry raised a glass of ouzo. 'I would like to propose a toast to Harry's Bar and ...' He smiled proudly. 'To introduce you all to my daughter.' He pulled her towards him and kissed her on the forehead.

He raised his glass and then his voice. 'Nyla.'

Their initial response was a shocked silence. Although they had heard Harry it took them by surprise, but within a few seconds they all raised their glasses and cheered loudly. The noisy chatter that followed continued for several minutes.

Harry took his time to reach out and kiss Nyla on the cheek.

Ben smiled to Nyla. 'I think I'm going to like it here.'

She was stunned.

Ben continued, with a wide smile. 'Your father has offered me a job.' He paused. 'Well, at least until I move on again.'

Nyla smiled back at him and nodded before sipping her wine.

Ben felt relieved and took his time to look around what would be his home for the foreseeable future. The bar had so many unusual touches. The rear mirrored wall was covered with rows of different sized tarnished spoons which started a foot above the table and up to the black timber beams on the ceiling. The remaining stuccoed walls were painted off-white and virtually every inch of them were covered with old paintings in heavy wooden frames. Harry had spent months scouring flea markets and second-hand shops buying up everything that was cheap enough and conveyed anything resembling old Cyprus. He obtained his tables and chairs in the same way and even visited houses that had been sold to ex-pats before they were cleared. He stripped the furniture down and stained it in rustic colours, allowing the grain and texture of the timber to show through. The timber floor was also unusual. Harry had been fortunate to obtain, totally free, the floor of a 1960's sports centre – providing he removed it, he did, and took his time to re-lay it. He carefully selected the recycled hardwood timber for the bar counter, which he machined into unusual profiles before treating it with a light cherry stain and sealing it. He hung second-hand industrial warehouse lights above the counter and backlit the rows of optics. He then spent weeks searching for armchairs and settees that had seen better days. Once they had been re-covered they looked as good as new. He carefully positioned the settees and armchairs at one end of the bar beneath subdued lighting. Every table inside the bar had a laminated menu and price list suspended from the ceiling by elastic so when the customers wanted to order, they reached up and pulled them down. They loved the idea and found it hilarious when the menu sprang up again.

Julian Stephens walked away from the bar and out onto the quiet of the terrace. He reached into his pocket, pulled out his mobile and looked at the number on the screen. He looked around surreptitiously before he answered. 'Hello.'

As he listened to the caller his face quickly ebbed of all colour. He sighed heavily as he clicked the phone and slipped it back into his trouser pocket.

CHAPTER SEVEN

Think Twice

In the very dark night, a small motorboat carrying two men made its way towards another boat in the harbour. One of the two shadowy figures climbed on board and rifled through the boat, checked the fuel cans and pulled out two full ones. He passed them to his accomplice who loaded them onto their boat. They pulled quietly away and made for another boat before disappearing into the night.

As dawn broke, Harry stopped along the cliff path and filled the rucksack with approximately 15kg of the larger stones. He gauged the weight and added two smaller stones before he hauled the bag onto his back and continued his daily ritualistic five mile run along the rocky coastal path.

When the army medics and specialists told him he would be confined to a wheelchair for the rest of his life, it was one of the many punishing regimes he pursued to gradually recover, against all odds, from his horrific injuries.

He panted heavily as he ran down towards the deserted beach that would soon be crowded with tourists. He stopped near an outcrop of rocks, removed the rucksack, and stripped off. He dived in and swam out to sea. Forty five minutes later Harry, looking refreshed and rejuvenated, tracked back along the path towards the harbour. He heard the sound of a racing engine and looked out to sea. He stood for a few minutes and watched the speedboat towing a parasail high above it as it followed the coastline.

The bar was busy with tourists and locals eating breakfast. Nyla moved happily between the tables, clearly enjoying her work. Harry and Ben were busy cleaning his boat, preoccupied with the music that boomed out of the radio, unaware of anything or anyone around them.

Nyla appeared on the quay. She mouthed something to them but they didn't hear her.

Harry motioned to Ben to turn down the music.

He obliged with a groan and instead turned it off.

Nyla turned towards them and shouted. 'Do you two want coffee?'

'I didn't think you'd ever ask,' replied Harry, with a mischievous grin.

Ben nodded in agreement. 'Two sugars for me please.'

Harry motioned to Ben to turn on the radio.

Ben shot him the broadest of smiles as he flicked it back on and turned it up even louder than before. As he gyrated to the dance music he took in his idyllic surroundings, the clear blue sky, the warm sun and the azure blue sea.

Pure bliss.

Julian leaned on the balcony of his luxury apartment and looked towards the sun-kissed harbour, the promenade and

Harry's Bar, before gazing out across the Mediterranean. With his mind elsewhere he was deep in thought as he sipped his coffee.

His wife, Patricia, holding a glass of golden liquor, tripped as she joined him on the balcony. 'Oops,' she slurred.

Julian turned to look at her. 'Isn't it a little early to be drinking?' He didn't hide his disgust. 'I've only just had breakfast.'

'Now …' she emphasised. 'I'm having mine.' She smirked at him and took a huge gulp of the liquor.

Julian's mobile pinged. He walked across to the table and picked it up. He checked it and looked across at Patricia, his face ashen and shocked. 'I'm going out,' he said, checking his watch. 'I should be back in time for lunch.' He paused and glared at his wife. 'Assuming you're compos mentis when I get back.'

Patricia garbled her reply as she took another huge swig from the glass and emptied it. 'Fine … that's just fine.'

She stood and rocked unsteadily.

Julian pushed past her and rushed down the stairs to the underground garage. Minutes later, with tyres screeching, he drove out of the garage in his red, open topped, classic 1968 E-type Jaguar.

While Ben finished polishing the veneered mahogany inside the cabin of the boat, Harry sat reading the Greek newspaper. After closing it he reread the headlines on the front page.

"THIEVES STEAL FUEL FROM LOCAL BOATS."

Ben looked across at Harry and coughed to gain his attention.

Harry looked up at him.

Ben asked. 'Why have you called your boat *Zero?*' He scratched his head and continued. 'It doesn't mean anything.'

Harry lowered the newspaper and grinned. 'That's right ... absolutely nothing,' he said, raising his hand regally.

Ben shot him a puzzled look. It took a few seconds for Harry's answer to dawn on him. 'Ah ... that's cool.' He grinned and nodded. 'Really cool – that's clever,' he said, laughing to himself.

Harry tutted and shook his head before he reread the headline story in his paper.

Julian raced along the harbour and, after speeding onto the breakwater, braked hard when he reached the first of the bar tables and chairs. He slammed the car door, pushed past Mama who was delivering another of her huge and now famous English breakfasts to a group of English tourists, and marched towards Harry's boat.

Harry lowered his newspaper, looked up at him and finished his espresso. 'Morning, Julian,' he said. 'Looks like another nice day.'

Julian ignored him, preferring to mumble to himself.

Harry, sensing Julian's indifference, passed Ben his empty cup and wiped his dirty hands on his jeans before he leapt effortlessly off the boat. He stood on the breakwater and tilted his head to one side. 'A bit early to see you here, eh, Julian?' He paused and grinned. 'But as you can see ...' He smiled with pride and spread his arms to emphasise the large number of tourists eating breakfast. 'We're open,' he said, with the widest of smiles. He took his time to study Julian and looked him up and down. 'You look like shit. Been up all night?'

'Is it that obvious?' replied Julian, timidly as he tried to hide his blushes.

'You dirty bastard. You *have* been up all night.' Harry laughed loudly and slapped Julian across his shoulder. 'Good luck to you, that's what I say.' He chuckled to himself. 'It's alright if you still have the stamina at your age.' Harry looked across to Ben, who was climbing onto the quay, and shouted across to him. 'Ain't that right, Ben?'

Ben ignored him and walked towards the bar to wash his dirty hands.

When he realised Nyla had heard Harry, Julian suddenly looked uncomfortable and rubbed his fingers nervously on his right thigh.

'Nyla, can you bring us a couple of coffees?' asked Harry, pointing to the table farthest from the bar. 'We'll be over there.'

Nyla nodded and danced towards the bar.

Julian and Harry sat at the shaded table in silence. Harry finally lost his patience and spoke firmly. 'So, come on Julian, what the *hell* is this all about?'

Julian reluctantly passed Harry his mobile phone and trembled as he showed him the photos and text.

When Nyla reappeared with the tray, Harry discreetly slid the phone into the palm of his hand, rested it on the table, and waited while she took the coffee from the tray.

Nyla spoke in Greek. 'Will that be all?'

Harry said, 'Yeah. Thanks. That's fine.'

Nyla could feel the tension and after nodding nervously walked briskly away.

Julian stroked the tablecloth anxiously while Harry reread the text. He finally laid the mobile on the table and pushed

Julian's cup and saucer towards him. He smirked at Julian as he picked up his coffee. 'Is this shit for real?' He looked out across the bay to allow himself time to think. He finally turned back to face Julian. 'If it is, you've got a lot of bother.' He sipped at his coffee and considered the possibilities. He placed the empty cup in the saucer and exhaled before gazing directly at the now trembling Julian. 'How long ago was that taken?'

Julian sniffed. 'A couple of years,' he said. He reached for his cup but left it in the saucer as he continued. 'Pat was back in the UK.' He stifled his reply and coughed. 'I met ...' He pointed at the picture and tapped it. 'Well ...' He blushed. 'She thought *I* was wonderful.' He grabbed his cup and gulped at the coffee. Some of the dregs at the bottom of the cup reached his mouth. He spluttered as he spat them into his white hand-kerchief. 'I know.' He swallowed nervously. 'Don't even say it, Harry.' He held up his hands in submission and shook his head. 'There's no fool like an old fool, right?'

Harry's reply was unexpected and Julian was clearly taken aback.

Harry continued. 'No. Good luck to you, Julian. But ...' He cleared his throat. 'What I want to know is ...' He sighed. 'Why have they waited until now?' He pushed his chair back onto two legs. 'What are you up to, Julian? Does Patricia know?'

Julian played nervously with his fingers. 'Well ...'

'Do you have any idea who would do this?' asked Harry, with a note of seriousness in his voice.

Julian screwed up his face. 'Erm, no.' He couldn't hide his dejection and shook his head. 'I've no idea.'

Harry closed his eyes and contemplated for a few seconds

before letting his chair drop back onto four legs with a loud thud. 'Listen, Julian ...' He paused to think before continuing with renewed enthusiasm in his voice. 'I don't know if I can help but if you don't give me some answers you may as well go to Zavos.' He leaned across the table and lowered his voice. 'The island's too small to hide something like this. It's got to get out sooner or later.'

Julian picked up his empty cup, looked into it and sniffed. 'That's what I expected you to say.'

Harry bit at his bottom lip. 'Can you leave your mobile with me?'

Julian frowned as he placed his empty cup back in the saucer.

Harry continued. 'Julian. You need to let me have it. Get yourself a new one – a pay as you go.'

Julian reluctantly slid his mobile across the table. Harry slipped it into his waistcoat pocket and pushed himself up. 'Let me have your new number as soon as you get it.'

'Sure.'

'Leave it with me, Julian. I'll see what I can do.'

Julian dropped his shoulders, walked dolefully back to his car and drove off.

Before Harry could get up, a white sports car raced along the breakwater and braked hard, stopping a few inches from his table.

Xanthi jumped out of the car and rushed towards him. 'Who do you think you are? My daughter's with you less than a week and she ... she's...' She shook her head fitfully. 'She's kidnapped!'

Harry raised his hands in submission. 'Hang on, Xanthi –'

'Call yourself a father? Trouble seems to follow you doesn't it, Harry Clark?' She paused and tried to anticipate his reply.

There was none.

'I still don't know why I married you,' she said, as she flicked at her razor cut shoulder length blond hair, with her left hand.

Harry took a moment and studied her body-hugging yellow cotton dress and tried to remember her delicious naked body. He took her arm and smiled to himself as he walked her to the boat. He took his time to answer. 'If it was that bad why did you never divorce me?' he said, with a mischievous grin.

He waited for her reply.

There wasn't one.

Harry continued. 'And you still call yourself, Mrs Clark?' He smirked at her and spoke in Greek. 'Is it the British passport?'

'Shut up, Harry,' she said. She sighed heavily. 'We both know you were married to the fucking army. Why try to fool me now?'

Harry conceded with a nod and a murmured grunt.

Xanthi forced a smile. 'Look. If you're going to be here for a while ...' She was interrupted as Nyla walked across to the boat, gave each of them a nervous smile, and passed Harry a tray with two coffees.

Xanthi looked up at her and smiled.

'Thanks, love,' said Harry.

Xanthi blew Nyla a kiss. 'Are you alright, darling?'

'Course I am, Mum.' She looked at Harry and smiled. 'I love it here,' she said, shaking her ponytail.

Xanthi shot Harry a stern look and finally continued. 'We ought to at least try to get on for her sake, didn't we?'

Harry said, 'Of course we do. We need to get on.' He smiled. 'I haven't got a problem with that.'

'Fine,' said Xanthi. She flicked her head back provocatively before she reached across and took a cigarette from the packet in his waistcoat pocket.

Harry lit it before taking one for himself.

'Nyla told me what happened.'

Harry nodded. 'Course.'

She took a drag and expelled a thick cloud of smoke. 'And who the hell is Stryker?'

He looked at her intensely. 'That was a previous life.' He made a big deal of lighting his cigarette and took a deep drag. 'Do you have any idea what it was like?'

She shook her head.

He exhaled as he spoke. 'Hate can go so far –'

'Tell me.'

'It was a lifetime ago –'

'But it came back again didn't it? In that warehouse?'

Harry rubbed at the stubble on his chin. 'Yes. It did.'

'And *our* daughter saw it.'

Harry sighed.

Xanthi said, 'She's still a child. How do you think she felt hearing that about her father, someone she never knew?'

'I know.' He sighed heavily. 'Seeing Malik again brought it all back to me. I remembered. I was in a very dark place.' He reflected as he sipped at his coffee. 'Do you know I was consumed by the hate and anger?' He reflected again as he exhaled. 'And revenge. And then I realised they were one and the same.'

Xanthi looked at him. 'I'm sorry.' She shook her head. 'But I don't understand any of that.' She tapped her ash into the makeshift ashtray – an empty beer bottle. 'I'll tell you what.'

He mouthed to her. 'What?'

'I hated you for such a long time.' She reflected on what she'd said. 'Yes, a very long time.'

Harry briefly closed his eyes and waited.

She continued. 'But do you know what?' She smiled at him. 'I don't anymore.'

Harry partially opened his eyes and watched her.

She shook her head and looked across at Nyla who was laughing and joking with a group of customers. Xanthi continued. 'It was a long time ago now.'

Harry reached out, touched her hand, and nodded. 'It was.' He spoke in a very soft voice. 'Why not come for dinner one evening.'

'I'd like that,' she said.

She finished her cigarette and pushed it into the bottle.

CHAPTER EIGHT

Sign of the Times

Nyla was taking an order from a couple of tourists sitting in the shade. She looked up when she saw the silver Saab 920 convertible pull up. Nichole Mouzie jumped out and walked confidently along the breakwater towards the bar.

Nyla repeated the tourists' order and turned to Nichole. 'Good morning.'

'Morning,' said Nichole.

'You're the reporter – from the paper?'

Nichole nodded confidently.

'Didn't I see you at the bar the other evening?'

She nodded.

'Coffee?' asked Nyla.

'Please.'

Nichole sat at one of the tables nearest to the sea and took out her notebook and pen.

Nyla placed the coffee and a glass of water on the table and paused. 'I like your top.'

Nichole replied with a smile. 'Thanks. It's old.'

'Old?'

'Well ...' Nichole blushed. 'Last year.'

'Oh.'

Nichole looked past Nyla. 'Is Harry around?'

'Oh, yeah. He's on his boat with my mother.'

Nichole looked very surprised. 'Your Mother?'

Nyla smiled. 'It's a very long story.'

Nichole looked at her with a discerning grin and nodded. 'Mmm ...'

Harry helped Xanthi off his boat and pretended to read his newspaper while he watched her walk towards her car.

Nichole waited for Xanthi to get into her car, picked up her coffee and made to stand.

'I wouldn't go over for a minute,' said Nyla.

'Is that right?' she said, tetchily. She ignored Nyla and ambled towards the boat.

Harry was already into his second newspaper, concentrating on the latest news from the UK.

'Hi, Harry. Did you get my message?'

Harry looked up and smiled. 'Hello, Nichole.'

She pulled a face as she repeated her question. 'Did you get my message?'

'What?' He mumbled to himself as he finally realised what she'd said. He pulled his mobile from his waistcoat pocket and checked it. 'Ah ... yeah.' He waved the English newspaper at her. 'But as you can see I've been a little preoccupied this morning,' he said, pointing towards Xanthi as she drove away.

Nichole grinned impatiently.

'So what can I do for you?' he asked.

'Have you seen the paper?'

Harry helped her onto his boat and picked up the local newspaper.

'Well ... I've read it. Why do you ask?'

Nichole placed her coffee on the seat, reached across, took the paper from him, and showed him the front page. She tapped repeatedly at the headline. 'That.'

Harry looked up at her and smiled. 'Your story?'

Nichole grinned. 'Yeah, that's *one* of mine.' She traced the headlines with her index finger. 'And there are a couple of features inside, fashion and dining.' She opened the paper and fanned the pages. 'And a few other bits as well as the advertising sections in the Paphos Times.'

Harry looked at her mockingly.

Nichole's attitude suddenly changed. 'Harry, this is Cyprus – not London. We don't have the luxury of a team of reporters working on *one* story for weeks on end.'

'That's fair enough,' he said, brusquely.

Nichole finished her coffee and looked towards the bar. She held up the magazine. 'I could do a feature on you, and your place, if you want me to?'

'No way,' said Harry. Without taking a breath he pointed at the magazine. 'I don't want my face splashed all over that.'

Nichole grinned. 'Something to hide from a previous life, eh, Harry?'

'Maybe – maybe not,' he said. 'Everyone has something to hide.' He paused. 'Even you, Nichole.' He leaned back and looked her up and down.

She was clearly thrown by his comment and turned away.

Harry raised his hand to Nyla and motioned for two more coffees. He knew his comment had the desired effect so he smiled and continued. 'OK, so why the message?' he asked, tapping his mobile.

She regained her composure and continued. 'I wondered if you had any idea who was stealing the fuel from the boats. Have you seen anything?'

Harry looked at her blankly.

Nichole continued. 'The story?'

'Oh, right.' He smirked. 'Front page headlines. Nah.' He shook his head. 'I can see why they're doing it – fuel prices are crazy now.' He screwed up his face. 'Nah – I dunno.' He sipped his coffee. 'Have you spoken to Zavos?'

'Zavos?' Nichole laughed loudly. 'Are you serious? He's a waste of space.'

Harry returned her laugh. 'Well, there you have it.' He smiled broadly. 'He'll get 'em. It might take a while but ...' He didn't finish the sentence. Instead, he stood as he finished his coffee.

Nichole took the hint and as she stood he helped her onto the quay.

'Good luck, Nichole. Keep at it. Watch out for your master criminals,' he said mockingly.

Nichole called back to him. 'You could be next, Harry.'

Harry raised his arms derisively and returned to his news-paper.

While the last few locals and tourists enjoyed their final drink of the evening, Harry worked in the dimly lit room at the rear of the bar. Sunshine Radio, the local English radio station, was playing and subconsciously he moved to the music. This was Harry's workshop – his domain – only he could enter. It was crammed with his retained Special Forces gear and his old faithful, a rucksack, which hung in pride of place on the wall. He connected Julian's mobile to his laptop and tapped at the keys. He carefully studied the screen and tapped at the keyboard again.

It was a beautiful morning and as Harry and Ben made their way along the coast the boat began to shudder. The engine spluttered and, as Harry tapped animatedly at his fuel gauge, they glided to a silent halt.

Harry shook his head in disbelief and continued to rap at the fuel gauge. 'Ben, under there you'll find a couple of cans.' He pointed at the hatch. 'Can you pass them out to me?' He rechecked Mama's shopping list while Ben pulled back the wooden hatch.

Ben searched the rest of the storage area. 'There's nothing here, Harry.'

'Come on Ben … use your bloody eyes.'

Ben continued to search beneath the seats, the lockers and cupboards. 'Harry … I already told you, there's nothing here.'

Harry jumped forward and reached into the storage area. 'Bloody hell,' he raged. 'Those thieving bastards – have done me too.'

It was two hours before they made it to the quayside and were able to refuel at the jetty before buying everything on Mama's extended list at the market.

Julian sat at the table listening to the BBC world news. His new mobile rang. He picked it up. 'Hello.' He listened and nodded before he clicked it off and slid it into his trouser pocket. 'I'm going out,' he said.

His wife slurred. 'So what's new?'

*   *   *

Harry was sitting at a table reading the newspaper when Julian drove up to the bar, sprung eagerly out of his car and rushed towards him.

'Morning, Harry – good news?' he asked enthusiastically.

'Sit down, Julian.' He looked towards the bar and shouted. 'Can we have a couple of coffees out here?'

Nyla replied from inside. 'Coming up.'

Julian demonstrated his impatience by the erratic movement of his left leg. 'Well ...' He looked at Harry and waited. Harry didn't accommodate him and he continued. 'You said you had something for me,' asked Julian, impatiently.

'Relax, Julian. You may not want to hear this –'

'Look ... if it's money, Harry. I can sort it.'

Harry nodded. 'Fine, but will you just sit down and listen.'

Reluctantly Julian obliged and gave Harry his undivided attention.

Harry continued. 'The calls are coming from here on the island and I'm close to finding out where.'

Julian gushed. 'Well, surely that's it then?'

'The way they've set this up ...' Harry screwed up his face '... is very professional. They know what they're doing and it won't be that easy. They are bouncing the calls around the satellites and back onto the island.' Harry grinned broadly and continued. 'But as I said, I've almost sussed how they're doing it –'

'Look – whatever it costs I just want this to *stop*.' He took a huge breath and spoke as he exhaled. 'Once and for all.'

Nyla brought the coffee and placed it neatly on the table. They briefly looked up and acknowledged her with half smiles and then immediately turned away.

Julian didn't hide his desperation. 'You've got to help me, Harry,' he spluttered.

'All right, Julian. I'll do what I can but I've got my own problems to sort out now.'

CHAPTER NINE

After Midnight

The bar was closed and the quay was silent. The small room at the rear of the bar was dimly lit and cluttered with tools, bottles and electronic equipment. Harry mixed a concoction of several powders in a large bottle and carefully tapped it into two red jerry cans. He carefully added the diesel and screwed on the caps. He cautiously checked the area before he crept through the shadows and carried the cans towards his boat. He carefully placed them in the rear of the boat, covered them with a tarpaulin, and leapt back onto the quay.

Julian and Harry cruised along the coast. 'All right Harry this had better be good. Couldn't we have done this on land?'

Harry replied. 'Julian, let's get one thing straight. This is your problem and if you want to finish it then it has to be my way. I'm not getting myself killed for you or anyone else.'

Julian spluttered. 'Killed? Is it that bad?' he said, as he broke into a sweat.

'If they've gone to the trouble of getting hold of those photos and setting this thing up they won't just go away again.' As he drank his beer he pondered briefly. 'Well, that is until they've taken you for as much as they dare.'

'What?'

Harry reflected. 'Well ... or until they've got what they came for.'

Julian trembled with anger. 'All right, Harry ... whatever you want to do ... just tell me.'

'OK,' said Harry. 'We'll send them a text and ask what they want ... and then we wait.' He looked hard at Julian. 'Are you alright with that?'

'If you can stop this ...' Julian looked at him despairingly. 'Erm ... Make this shit go away. That's fine.'

Julian's mobile rang once. Harry checked it and read the text twice. He reached for his mobile and dialled.

Julian answered. 'Hello, Harry.' He nodded excitedly as he listened. 'Yeah ... I know it's two in the morning.' He rubbed his tired eyes. 'Fifty thousand ... is that right?' He walked out onto the balcony and looked up into the moonlit sky. 'Yeah ... that's fine. I'll be there.' He paused. 'Oh, and Harry ... I'm relying on you.'

Harry clicked the phone.

An hour later a small boat made its way across the harbour.

Suddenly it exploded.

Harry was in bed, asleep. A hand reached towards his throat and grabbed him. Immediately the bedroom was illuminated by flickering flashlights. Harry briefly covered his eyes and as he uncovered them he took in what was going on.

The lights revealed Zavos and several policemen pointing their handguns in Harry's direction.

Zavos screamed out. 'Get up, Harry.' He paused. 'Slowly now.' He pointed his gun towards Harry's head and stepped back. 'Slowly.'

Harry stared at them in total disbelief and forced a laugh. 'Come on, Zavos. Is this some kind of joke?'

'It is no joke, my friend,' said Zavos. He stepped back. 'Now get dressed.'

Harry glared back at them as he took his time to pull on his jeans, t-shirt and waistcoat, then slipped his feet into his deck shoes.

Harry sat on one side of a heavily scratched table and Zavos, accompanied by another man in uniform, sat on the other side, while two armed policemen stood guard anxiously in front of the closed door.

Tensions were high.

Harry shook his head. 'I don't know anything about it –'

Zavos slammed his fists on the table. 'The next time ... somebody could get killed.' He paused. 'You know what that means?'

'Erm,' mumbled Harry, as he nodded slowly. He looked at the clock on the wall and made to stand but the two armed policemen rushed forward and forced him back into his chair.

The clock on the wall showed 10:35.

Zavos noticed Harry looking up at it.

'That's why we're here, to see if you do,' he said, as he thumbed through his notebook. 'Tell me. What is it, Harry?'

Zavos waited.

He looked towards the clock. 'Since when have you been interested in the time?' He paused. 'You chose to come to our wonderful island like all the other English ...' He grinned at his plain-clothed colleague sitting next to him. He continued. 'To get away from time – right?'

Harry shrugged his shoulders.

Zavos looked at the contents in the middle of the table, taken from Harry's pockets, and continued. 'And why do you have two mobile phones? Eh?'

Harry shrugged again.

'Is it drugs, Harry?'

Harry slammed his fists on the table. 'Fuck you, Zavos.' He grinned. 'You know I wouldn't get into that shit.'

'Are you sure, Harry?'

Julian stood on the quayside and looked nervously around as he repeatedly checked his watch. He spoke under his breath. 'Damn you, Harry ... where the hell are you?'

Julian checked his mobile and pushed it back into his pocket before climbing awkwardly into the waiting motorboat. He checked the details on his phone 'That way,' he said, as pointed towards the headland.

As the motorboat made its way out of the harbour Julian rechecked the location on his mobile, then looked around at the coloured flags marking the lobster pots. He rechecked the phone again before pointing towards a yellow striped flag. 'Over there,' he said.

They made their way to the striped flag. Julian reached over and pulled up the lobster pot. He placed the waterproof bag inside and looked around before he reluctantly dropped it back into the sea. He was sweating profusely as he spoke to the boatman. 'Let's go. Let's get away from here.'

The boat made its way along the coast and back towards the harbour.

An hour later an unmarked motorboat pulled up to the striped yellow flag, one of the occupants grabbed the pot, removed the bag, and it pulled away.

Harry walked out of the police station, tugged at his waist-coat, felt the mobile phones in the pockets and made his way towards the taxi rank. He muttered instructions to the driver as he got in. As the taxi drove away Harry looked back towards the police station, clenched his fists, and cursed Zavos under his breath.

Julian's mobile rang.

Harry pulled it from his pocket but didn't speak.

'Well, Harry? Talk about keeping a low profile. Where were you?' He coughed. 'Did you get them?' invited Julian.

Harry spoke in an unusually subdued voice. 'No, no Julian.' He looked out of the taxi window and sighed. 'No. I didn't –'

'What?' Julian seethed. 'So where are you?'

'That bastard, Zavos arrested me –'

'He did what? I thought you said you'd keep him out of it.'

'Yeah ... I know.' Harry didn't hide his frustration. He let out a huge sigh. 'Meet me at the bar and I'll explain.'

Ben was taking an order at one table while Nyla cleared and wiped down another. She dropped her cloth and plates on the table and rushed towards Harry as he climbed out of the taxi.

'Where have you been? You could have left a message or ... or, told somebody.' She hugged him. 'I mean –'

'There was no way I could do anything. The police dragged me out of bed –'

'Police?'

'Well, Zavos anyway.'

'Wha ... ?'

'Don't worry. It's sorted.'

Julian drove up to the bar and walked briskly towards Harry and Nyla.

Nyla spoke in Greek. 'It's got something to do with *him* hasn't it?'

Harry motioned to her to leave. 'Ah.' He waved her question away with his hand. 'Get us a couple of beers, eh?' He forced a smile. 'That's a good girl.'

Nyla muttered under her breath as she stormed off.

Harry and Julian sat at the far end of the bar and slowly worked their way through several bottles of beer.

'Listen, Julian. Trust me. I'm not too worried about today. If they got away with it once they will try it again.' He grinned. 'And ... the next time?' He cursed under his breath. 'I'll get them,' he said, with determination in his voice.

Julian looked concerned. 'What about the money?' He paused. 'I suppose –'

Julian's mobile pinged. Harry reached into his waistcoat pocket, pulled it out and carefully read the text. He smiled broadly. 'Well, well, well. I told you they'd come back for more.'

'Already?' gasped Julian.

'With respect Julian, they know they've got a real sucker – a rich one at that.'

Julian shook his head with a combination of embarrassment and disgust.

Harry worked in his workshop throughout the night, fine tuning small electronic devices and testing the equipment. The next morning Julian, Ben and Harry sat on his boat a short distance from the breakwater.

'So you all know what we're doing?' asked Harry.

Ben and Julian nodded and answered simultaneously. 'Yeah.'

'This might be our one and only chance. So don't mess up.' He reflected and nudged his elbow hard into Julian's ribs. 'Well?'

Julian couldn't hide his mixed emotions and scowled at Harry as he rubbed at his bruised ribs. 'Course I do.'

Harry continued. 'Make sure you take the boatman for a drink and keep him there until I call you. I don't trust anyone now.'

Julian nodded.

Harry fired up the engine and raced back towards his bar.

Julian walked out of the bank carrying a briefcase and met the new boatman at the Harbour Side taverna. While he sipped at his coffee he continually checked his watch. His mobile pinged. They walked across the quay and climbed awkwardly into the motorboat. He raised his hand and the boat pulled away. He turned away from the driver and as he removed the money from the briefcase he counted it before sliding it into the waterproof bag.

Julian's boat continued out into the Mediterranean and made its way towards the marker flags. They stopped when they reached their destination. Julian pulled up the same yellow and black striped flag and placed the waterproof bag into the lobster pot. He deliberated for a split second and then dropped it. 'You'd better be around this time, Harry,' he said, cursing under his breath.

He sighed heavily as he looked around at the empty expanse of sea. Unable to hide his reluctance he spoke to the boatman. 'Let's go,' he said, as he flicked his head towards land. The launch turned and made for the harbour.

Harry, wearing a headset with a microphone, towed a para-sailer along the coast. He looked up. 'Are you OK? Can you see anything?'

'Not yet, Harry. Just keep her steady,' said Ben. He had never been a good traveller and pressed gently at his stomach and swallowed, in an attempt to relieve the nausea.

Harry continued along the coast towing Ben high above him.

The unmarked motor launch arrived at the black and yellow striped flag.

'I can see something,' shouted Ben. He watched as one of the occupants hauled up the lobster pot, removed the bag and pulled slowly away. 'They've got it,' he screamed. He was unable to contain his excitement as the adrenalin raced through his whole body. 'Yes, Harry. They've got it!'

Harry grinned to himself. 'That's great,' he said.

The unmarked motor launch accelerated towards the coast.

'Hold tight, I'm going closer,' said Harry. He turned and shadowed the motor launch.

The blackmailers had no idea Harry was following them and, gaining all the time, he finally caught up with them a few hundred yards from the harbour.

While "Zero" made its way towards the breakwater, Harry let Ben take the wheel and reached for his mobile. 'Hi, Julian –'

'Did you get them?' gushed Julian.

'Meet me at the bar in an hour and a half,' said Harry, flicking his mobile before Julian could ask anything else.

Harry was working behind the bar serving drinks to a group of tourists when Julian rushed in and made directly for him. Harry raised his hand, opened his palm, and motioned to Julian to wait.

Julian reluctantly sat on the bar stool and tapped his fingers impatiently.

Harry handed the customers their drinks and turned to Julian.

'Well?' asked Julian excitedly.

Harry grunted and spent the next few minutes wiping down the bar before handing Julian a beer.

Julian couldn't hide his impatience and raised his voice. 'And the money?'

Harry shot him an incongruous look. 'Yeah, we got it.'

Julian let out a huge sigh of relief. 'Excellent.' He took a deep breath and exhaled before continuing. 'So who are they?'

Harry pointed to the darkened corner table at the far end of the bar and the person sitting in an armchair.

Julian grabbed his beer and with obvious trepidation walked towards the table and the perpetrator. When he reached the table he pulled his head back in total shock. 'You?' exclaimed a stunned Julian, his face a mask of confusion. He turned to Harry and released his pent up anger. 'Is this some sort of sick joke?'

Harry shook his head slowly as he mouthed every word. 'It's no joke, Julian.'

Patricia looked up at her husband and burst into tears. "I'm so sorry, Julian,' she said softly. 'I know it was cruel to put you through all this but ...' She wiped erratically at her eyes and smudged her eye liner across her cheeks. 'But I didn't know what else to do – '

'DO!' screamed Julian. He shook his head erratically as he tried to come to terms with the shock. He took in a massive gulp of air followed immediately by a huge swig of beer. 'I don't believe you planned all this on your own.' He slumped into the armchair opposite his wife and took another swig of beer. 'I just don't believe it.' He exhaled and shook his head wildly. 'I mean.' He tried to choke back the shock before clearing his throat. 'How could you stoop so low?' He swallowed before he continued. 'Robbing your own husband?'

Patricia reached out for his hand.

For a split second he froze, then glared at her before pulling his empty hand away.

Patricia continued. 'Julian, you let me down with that ghastly *whore*.' She collected her thoughts. 'Or ...' She swallowed hard. 'Have you already chosen to forget that?'

She took the photograph from her handbag and placed it on the table, turned it around and slid it across to him. Julian spluttered his wordless response and turned away from her. She took a large envelope from her handbag and slid it across the table. 'The money's all here.' She paused. 'Except a few hundred euros I used to pay for the men and the boat.' She opened the envelope and flicked through the notes. 'It is all here. Look.'

Julian turned away from his wife before speaking. 'How could you even think to do something like this?'

She reached across and tugged at his jacket. 'Do you know what it's like being married to a man ...' she looked directly at him, 'who only thinks about making money?' She looked at the photograph, reconsidered and continued in a softer voice. 'Well ... most of the time.'

He looked at her and wiped at his tearful eyes.

She could feel his humiliation. 'Tell me, Julian. Why do we stay together? Our marriage is a sham ... and most of the time ... you don't even know I'm around.'

Julian grimaced. 'What do you expect? These days you're always *pissed*.'

Patricia laughed loudly. 'Ah. But I don't *drink*.' She stood up. 'Don't you see? It was all part of –'

'Part of what?' he retorted angrily.

Patricia laughed as she spoke. 'I've been planning this for months.' She shook her head erratically and sat down. 'Some days, I really wanted to punish you.' She bit her bottom lip. 'I didn't have the nerve to go through with it.' She closed her eyes and swallowed. 'I could have left you ...' She took a handkerchief from her handbag and wiped away her tears. 'And gone back to England.' She could feel Julian mentally searching for the reason why she hadn't left him. She chose to release a smile and turned to Julian. 'But, do you know what?'

He screwed up his face and mouthed. 'What?'

He waited.

'I actually like it here,' she said, as her face radiated happiness.

Julian exhaled his relief. He nodded slowly as he agreed with her. 'Yeah.' He took several sips of his beer before he quizzed her in a soft trembling voice. 'How did you find out?'

She didn't want to hold back. 'When you've been married to someone as long as I have you get to know everything about them.' She smiled broadly. 'It was a real giveaway.' She giggled. 'It was so obvious. You were never very good with gadgets.' She sipped her drink for the first time.

He stared at the glass and silently quizzed her.

She passed the glass to him to taste.

He pushed it away.

'It's tonic water.' She giggled. 'Slimline – I hate alcohol.' She shuddered. 'Surely you know that?'

He blushed and nodded as he remembered. 'Um.'

She brushed it aside. 'Ah well.' For the first time, she appeared to relax and toyed with him. 'I'm surprised you can even use a mobile phone.' She laughed raucously. 'You can't work the remote control.' She suddenly realised how loud she had laughed and tried to hide her embarrassment by covering her mouth with her empty hand.

Julian ignored her ridicule. 'But you didn't do all this on your own? How could you?'

'Course not.' She straightened her loose fitting blouse, accentuating her large breasts. 'Erm – no.' She exhaled. 'I had help.' She paused. 'And it cost me.' She fiddled with the beer mat. 'Well, it cost ... *you.*'

Julian pointed at the open envelope of money on the table. 'But you said –'

'Well.' She took a deep breath and continued. 'The first fifty thousand euros anyway –'

Julian gagged and his whole body stiffened. 'Wha ... ?' He frowned as he straightened himself in his chair.

Patricia continued. 'Don't even think about it – they've already left the island.'

Julian held up his hands in submission before reaching across the table, hugging and kissing her.

For a few minutes they savoured the relief.

Still hugging her close, Julian turned towards the bar. 'Come on, Harry.' He waited for Harry to acknowledge him. 'Can we have those drinks now?'

'Champagne?'

'Nothing less,' he said contentedly.

Patricia looked over Julian's shoulder towards Harry and mouthed. 'One glass, please.'

CHAPTER TEN

On The Beach

It was an unusually cloudy day and most of the tourists had chosen to sit inside. The bar was buzzing. While Nyla cleared tables and Ben took orders at a noisy table of six, Harry sat working on his accounts, something that was alien to him. He hated figures but now he had to deal with it.

Ben acknowledged Nichole with a smile as she walked across to Harry's table.

'Morning, Harry,' said Nichole.

Harry looked over his new glasses and nodded.

'I hear Zavos arrested you,' she said, with a hint of a news story in her eyes.

Harry shrugged and removed his glasses. 'A misunderstanding ...' He huffed. 'That's all.'

Nichole spoke to him in Greek. 'You know what they say, Harry.' She then spoke in English. 'No fire without smoke.'

Harry laughed loudly. 'No smoke without fire.' He immediately knew he had offended her. He reached out and tapped her shoulder. 'I'm sure you were right the first time.'

She ignored his apology and left, but as she reached the end of the breakwater a delivery van reversed its way past her until it reached the first row of tables.

Two men got out. They opened the rear doors and struggled towards the bar with an upright piano. They stopped at the entrance and the driver called out. 'We have a delivery for Harry Clark.'

Harry acknowledged them from his table and called over to Ben. 'Here you are Ben – a present from Julian.'

Ben looked at the piano and shot Harry a puzzled look.

Harry laughed. 'And I hope you're as good as you said you were or you'll be looking for another job.'

Ben was better than he'd said. He could play anything, from singalong cockney tunes, classical and even the latest melodic chart songs. Each evening he cleverly changed the music to suit the clientele and, as well as Harry, they all loved it.

The bar was very busy. Harry busied himself behind the bar and served a customer while Zavos sat on a bar stool in front of him. Harry finished serving the customers, poured Zavos a Metaxa and handed him a bottle of beer.

Zavos emptied the brandy glass in one gulp before speaking. 'Harry, the illegal immigrants have been taken to a reception centre for asylum seekers at Kofinou village. He started on his beer and wiped the froth from his mouth. 'The judge of the District Court of Paphos, Christodoulos Christodoulou, will be talking to the media tomorrow and telling them that the traffickers.' He paused and took a huge slug of this beer. 'If they are found, they will be faced with offences of conspiracy to commit a crime, assistance to prohibited immigrants in the territory of the Republic of Cyprus, and … smuggling immigrants by sea.' He emptied the glass and slid it across to Harry. 'Harry, he also mentioned that anyone considered suitable for asylum status would be made aware of the decision within a minimum of ninety days, and if successful they will be issued with EU passports.'

Harry served another customer and turned to Zavos. Without refilling his glass, he grunted.

Zavos remained at the bar and his patience finally paid off when Harry refilled the brandy glass and slid another beer across to him.

While Ben played the piano, Nichole Mouzie leaned on his shoulders and intently watched his fingers as they magically danced on the keys. A group of English tourists squeezed around them and sang along – raucously and out of tune. They were on holiday and no one cared.

Zavos raised his voice, to be heard above the singing, and lifted his glass. 'Harry, a toast.' He managed a gash of a smile. 'And my many apologies for –'

At that precise moment a massive explosion out in the harbour reverberated around the building, rattling the glasses hanging above the bar.

The music and singing stopped immediately and Nichole raced through the door and stood on the edge of the break-water.

'Stay inside. There could be more,' shouted Harry.

'More?' asked the stunned Zavos.

The motorboat burned fiercely, illuminating the empty boats. Flames stretched high into the clear night sky and lit up Nichole's shocked face.

Harry followed Zavos outside and smiled. 'Got ya,' he said, under his breath.

Zavos turned to him. 'Maybe I was right after all?'

Harry grinned at him and whispered into his ear. 'Prove it.'

CHAPTER ELEVEN

Lovely Summer Day

Harry sat inside the bar reviewing the takings for the past few weeks. Deciding to have a break from coffee, he sipped at his herbal tea while he rechecked the spreadsheet on his laptop. 'Um,' he muttered, as he scratched his head. He walked into the kitchen, spoke to Mama, and then called out to Nyla. 'Come and sit down here for a minute.' She looked around at the occupied tables waiting to place their orders. Harry continued. 'Only for a minute, okay?'

She sat down next to him and sipped at his tea. 'Urgh.' She spat it into her cleaning cloth. 'Since when did you take sugar?' she quizzed.

He shot her a frivolous grin. 'Sometimes I feel I need it.'

'Why not try honey – it's good for you and much better than sugar.'

He chose to ignore her and instead, returned to his laptop.

Nyla fiddled with her order book and clicked her pen top while she waited for him to speak.

Harry rubbed thoughtfully at the bristles on his chin before eventually looking up at her. 'I've been checking the takings and Monday is our slowest day,' he said. He picked up his cup and put it back into the saucer without drinking. 'Any ideas?'

She screwed up her face. 'Erm, no. Why would I?'

'Shall I tell you?'

She nodded.

Harry continued. 'I think Monday is the first day when the tourists go out on excursions and trips. They've rested for the weekend and want to explore .'

She screwed up her face. 'Really?'

'Well, do you have a better reason?' he snapped.

She shook her head and craned her neck to get a better look out at the occupied tables.

Harry grinned at her focused concern. 'They're fine. They're on *holiday*. Why should they rush off?'

She appeared to relax but seconds later she made to stand.

Harry tugged gently at her arm.

'Well, I've made a decision to close ... Mondays –'

'What?'

He smiled at her. 'Only in the day, we'll reopen at seven. It will do us all good to have some time off.'

She forced a smile. 'Alright, let's try it. But you will need to make sure everyone knows or we'll lose business for the rest of the week.'

'I'm already on it. I'll run a chain along the front of the tables and put a sign on it, and we can place a note in all of the menus.' He thought. 'And we'll make sure to tell any new arrivals on Sunday.'

Nyla raced off towards the customers without answering him.

*   *   *

The following Monday, Ben, Nyla and Mama piled into "Zero". They made their way along the coast and dropped anchor a few hundred yards off Chlorakas Beach. Harry was the first to dive into the deep crystal clear water, followed by Ben and Nyla who frolicked and cavorted in the water beside the boat as they enjoyed the moment.

While Ben and Nyla lay on deck and dried off in the hot summer sun, Harry, wearing only his shorts, climbed over the side.

Nyla and Ben looked up and immediately noticed the horrific scars on his body. They each shared the shock and motioned to each other to remain silent.

Mama worked inside the wheelhouse and, protected from the sun, prepared lunch. She cut into chunky halloumi blocks, flavoured with tahini cheese and a small handful of chopped chives, before she uncovered a dish of cold fried chicken on wooden skewers with tangy slaw, pickles and flat bread. Also a selection of cold meats with tzatziki dip, cold rice and potatoes. Her final pièce de résistance was to produce a large bowl of Greek salad containing tomatoes, cucumbers, red onion, bell peppers, large chunks of feta cheese and olives, with oil and oregano drizzled on top of it.

Harry opened a bottle of red wine, a bottle of white wine and a pack of ice cold beers which he passed to Ben. After eating much of the food, they were about to stretch out on the deck when Mama magically produced a delicious Greek yogurt infused with vanilla essence, drizzled with honey, topped with walnuts and sprinkled with cinnamon.

Harry smiled to himself as he watched his new found "family" enjoying themselves together. 'I'm so pleased I decided to come back here, you know,' he said, contentedly.

Ben and Nyla, their mouths full of yoghurt, mumbled their pleased response.

That evening everyone seemed refreshed and, as always, the bar buzzed.

CHAPTER TWELVE

Starting Over

Nyla desperately wanted to help some of the immigrants and spent much of her spare time trying to get them released. She made a number of visits to Achim Kallidis, at the Aliens and Immigration Unit, and Zavos, at the Divisional Police Headquarters of Paphos. Their offices were located in a listed building dating from the beginning of last century, next to the Kennedy Square in the centre of Paphos. The two storied building had been constructed with local ashlar stone, and a unique tiled roof. The entire building was U-shaped with an inner atrium. After several more visits to the bustling and intimidating building, she had a lengthy telephone conversation with Achim Kallidis. He confirmed that passports would be issued to Haya and Nooda, the young Syrian girls, within a few days and once they had them they would be free to work on the island.

Nyla replaced the handset and found it hard to contain her excitement as she rushed out to Harry who was unloading groceries from his boat. 'They're going to release Haya and Nooda,' she said, finding it impossible to hide her excitement.

'What?'

'The two young girls – you know them, the trafficked immigrants.' The excitement in her eyes cut through Harry. 'Remember?' She tutted. 'How can you forget? I haven't stopped talking about them.'

'Yeah. So what?' he said, dismissively.

Nyla continued. 'Kallidis called to say that they now have passports so they can stay on the island and if we vouch for them they can work here.'

He shot her a confused look. 'What? *Here*? Work at the bar?'

'Why not?' she asked angrily.

Harry didn't hide his concern. 'We can't have any more people working here. If we do, we'll never make any money and then what do you think will happen?' he asked indignantly. 'You need to remember … the bar is a business,' he said, emphasising the last words.

She lowered her head and sobbed.

Harry moved close to her and after rearranging the bags in his arms – he nuzzled her. 'Look. They can stay with you in your room for a while and –'

'OK. I'll call Kallidis back,' said Nyla, eagerly pulling away.

Harry lost his balance and struggled with the bags. 'Hang on a minute. Let's just see how they get on –'

'Yeah – sure, Dad,' she said, enthusiastically.

Harry shook his head as he watched her race off towards the bar and the telephone.

Like all of their fellow trafficked Syrians, the two young girls had lost more than a third of their body weight. But by the time they were released from the immigration centre they were almost unrecognisable. Nooda and Haya rushed through the gates towards Nyla and Harry and took it in turns to forcefully hug them. Their transformation was incredible. They were almost back to their true weight; their smiles were breathtaking, their dark brown eyes were bright and their black hair gleamed in the sunlight.

The three girls chatted excitedly while Harry led them to the quayside and into his boat.

As they made their way across the harbour they couldn't contain their elation at being free at last. They nodded excitedly. They didn't stop talking as they revelled in their new found freedom and took in their beautiful surroundings for the first time.

Nooda reached into her pocket and pulled out her newly issued passport and a roll of euros. She looked at Harry. 'I kept them,' she said, with a smile. 'Thank you.'

Harry winked at her. 'Good girl. Keep it safe, eh?'

'Thank you, Harry,' said Haya. 'It will be good for the future.'

Harry initially talked to them in Arabic but within a few minutes they began to converse in Greek and English, something they had learned while at the processing centre. Harry explained that they could stay at the bar and share a room with Nyla and if they wished, could help out.

Nyla opened three cans of coca cola and handed one to each of them. They drank most of it before they finally sat back breathless. In silence, they took their time to enjoy the sun and celebrate their freedom.

Harry watched them physically relax and took a deep breath. 'Tell me girls, how you both came to end up here?' he asked softly.

They girls looked at each other and waited. Nooda sipped at her drink, wiped her mouth with the palm of her hand and after staring at Haya she spoke. 'I lived in Damascus. It was a wonderful city.' She reflected. 'I loved it.'

Harry nodded. 'It is.' He coughed. 'I mean … it was.'

Haya nodded wildly. 'Yeah, my father died and my mother was a widow.' She paused and looked out across the harbour. 'She died too.' She closed her eyes and took a sad breath. She continued. 'And I was left alone in the big city.'

Nooda interrupted her. 'My father is Haya's uncle so she came to live with us in Aleppo.'

Haya smiled broadly, reached out, and squeezed her hand.

Nyla threw Harry a satisfied grin but his reaction was that of deep concern.

Haya continued. 'We are very similar in our ages.' She looked at Nyla and pulled back her long hair from her face. 'Nineteen?'

Nooda smiled her agreement but her face was soon a combination of anger and sadness. 'In 2012, following the rebel attack on our part of the city – everything changed.'

Haya spoke. 'It was terrible, gunfire, fighting in the streets –'

'And then bombs …'

'Lots of bombs,' said Haya.

Harry lit a cigarette. 'East Aleppo, yeah?' He sighed heavily and closed his eyes. 'Hmm.'

'In a few weeks …' Nooda sighed heavily, '… it was unbearable.'

'Buildings being blown up – bombed and crashing down. Nowhere was safe,' said Haya.

Nooda struggled for breath. 'Everyone was fighting for control of our part of the city.' She shuddered. 'It was so dangerous.' She lowered her voice and swallowed hard. 'Sometimes they even used nerve gas,' she said, sorrowfully. She closed her eyes and shook her head in disgust.

Haya tried to raise the mood and, after hugging Nooda, she continued. 'Nooda's uncle finally helped us,' she said.

Nooda smiled at her as she wiped her eyes.

Haya continued. 'He traded the last of their Syrian pounds for American dollars and paid *them* to help us escape.'

'We travelled across Syria in trucks until we arrived at the Turkish border.'

'Then ...' Haya grimaced. 'We were forced into UN painted coaches –'

'They were.' Nooda struggled for the correct words. 'How do you say, a ... a disguise?'

'I can believe that,' cursed Harry. He drew on his cigarette. 'So you ended up on that rust bucket ...' They didn't understand him. 'Erm ...' He waved his arms around while he searched for the correct words. 'The old fishing boat ...'

'Yeah, the ship – it was terrible –'

'The smell ...' Nooda fought hard not to vomit. 'Urgh.'

They nodded and Harry continued. 'And you arrived here in Cyprus?'

Nyla changed the subject. 'You're safe now – with us. Yeah?'

They both looked towards her and smiled. They mouthed simultaneously. 'Thank you. Thank you very much.'

Nooda and Haya helped out at the bar, clearing tables, working with Mama, and shopping with Harry. Heads frequently turned as they walked through the market with Harry but he ignored it and made a show of his feelings for the girls. They immediately settled in and were almost indispensable as the late summer trade really took off and business at Harry's Bar boomed. Some evenings it was impossible to find a table and there was always a queue of young people wanting to relax and enjoy a drink in the hot tub.

The bar's success had its problems. Logoed towels disappeared every evening, so Harry began charging a ten euro deposit when anyone wanting to use the hot tub ordered their first drink. They still vanished, but he hadn't lost money, and it advertised his bar.

CHAPTER THIRTEEN

After Midnight

It was a beautiful morning. It was already warming up and Harry's Bar had a busy day ahead. Nooda and Haya were inside polishing the cutlery and glasses. Harry was on a ladder, replacing broken coloured lights beneath the grapevines. Nyla was sweeping the floor beneath the tables outside. Ben slid back the cover of the hot tub to open it up for the day. He looked inside and vomited violently.

Nyla rushed over to him and looked into the tub. She let out an earthshattering scream, which brought not only the girls from the bar but also Mama, Jane and Ray.

Harry slid down the ladder and looked over their shoulders.

'What the fuck?' he raged. He looked into the hot tub and shook his head wildly. 'OK, Ben put the cover back on!' He looked at the vomit beneath several of the tables. 'Get a bucket of water and add a couple of capfuls of bleach – no more ... and wash it down. Nyla set up the hose and when Ben's finished run a fine spray over the whole floor.' Harry looked up at the sun. 'Yeah, that'll dry in no time.' He clapped his large hands. 'Let's go.'

He jumped into his boat and pulled on his wellington boots. He grabbed a handful of bin liners, a bucket and a kids fishing net which had been left behind by a French boy several weeks earlier. He jumped onto the terrace and slid one bin liner inside the other before removing the lid from the hot tub. He took several photos on his mobile and pushed it deep into his waistcoat pocket. As he pulled on his rubber gauntlet gloves he exhaled with anger and talked to himself. 'Who the hell would do this?' he cursed. He looked towards the quay and took his time to take in the numerous bars that vied for their share of the tourist business. He stopped abruptly, checked his watch and shook his head as he reached into the bloody mess. He pulled out the carcass of a dog that had been left there overnight. Its stomach had been slashed open leaving its guts floating in the hot tub. 'The bastards,' he said, shaking his gloves. He let the bloody water drip off the carcass before dropping it into the bin liner. He then removed the larger lengths of the entrails by hand and fished out the remainder with the net. Attracted by the smell of the rotting flesh, flies started to buzz around his arms and face. He ignored them as he tied a knot in the bin liners and threw them into his boat. He used the bucket to remove the majority of the repulsive bloody sludge before reaching for the large plastic container of bleach and pouring it into the remaining liquid. He then drained it off and scrubbed like a madman. He paused briefly and shouted to Ben who was still cleaning up his mess. 'Ben, get a sign typed up and laminate it.'

Ben looked up at him, his face pale and confused.

Harry continued. 'Just type – OUT OF USE. Alright? And fix it securely to the hot tub cover.'

Ben nodded and returned to scrubbing the granite paving.

When he was satisfied that he had removed all signs of vomit and blood, he picked up his bucket. 'Who the hell would do this, Harry?' he asked, unable to hide his shock.

Harry looked across to him, rolled his bottom lip and slowly shook his head as he muttered obscenities to himself.

Ben sensed Harry's anger. He sighed heavily and raced towards the bar and the computer.

Nyla continued to hose down the paving and, suitably impressed with her efforts, she smiled to herself as she coiled up the hose.

The bar was expecting its busiest day of the summer and Harry knew someone had carefully chosen that day to sabotage it. The bar had been booked by a party of twelve from Newcastle for a surprise boozy lunchtime fortieth birthday party. Later in the afternoon a family was booked following the christening of a young English couple's baby girl. For the evening, Harry had arranged a Greek theme night, with party food and a three piece band, and was expecting several hundred people to attend, along with anyone else who may decide to come to the bar after walking along the quayside.

Harry finished scrubbing the last traces of blood from the hot tub and shouted to Nyla. 'Set up the party table down the end.' Still wearing his gauntlet gloves, he pointed to an area farthest from the hot tub. 'Tell the girls too.' He briefly closed his eyes in thought. 'And get them started on it now.' He turned on the tap and after refilling the hot tub he slid the cover across. He looked across to Nooda and Haya who were busying themselves setting up the party table. 'Don't forget the party poppers and balloons.'

Nooda and Haya nodded excitedly.

Harry joined them. He loved their enthusiasm and gently tapped each of them on the shoulder.

Throughout the day and late into the evening, Harry was unable to forget the earlier events and continued to take an interest in the other bars along the quayside, looking for any obvious clues as to who was responsible.

There weren't any.

He knew the sabotage was not a one off incident, but a warning, and the next time he was determined to be prepared.

The day was a massive success and that evening the busiest of the season. The bar took twice as much as usual and Harry made the decision to book the band every Tuesday and Thursday throughout August.

When everyone had gone and the bar was closed Harry sat on his boat, lit a cigarette, and sipped at a bottle of beer. He smiled to himself with relief that the perpetrator's efforts had been little more than a distraction, and pleased that no one had even mentioned the hot tub being out of action.

The next morning Harry phoned Zavos and invited him for coffee. He then asked everyone to come and sit down with him at a table near to the already clear and bubbling hot tub.

Nooda, Haya, Ben and Nyla looked at him with trepidation.

He looked at his watch. 'Come on, sit down,' he said, impatiently.

Reluctantly they sat down at the table and waited. Harry forced a reassuring smile. 'Don't look so worried. But after yesterday.' He let out a sigh of relief.' I think I need to give you a few pointers on your safety.'

They all nodded nervously back to him but relaxed when they saw Mama walk out with a tray of drinks. She put them on the table and left.

'OK. Yesterday ...' He looked towards the hot tub. 'Was a one-off,' he snapped. He didn't hide his anger. His whole body stiffened and as his hands tensed they were transformed into menacing white knuckled fists. He noticed everyone's fearful reaction as they pulled away from the table. He exhaled and after flexing his fingers he continued. 'And ... I will be making sure that it doesn't happen again.' He paused briefly and grinned. 'But there are some things I want you to think about.' He coughed and continued. 'A few pointers that may help you ... if you do ever need it.'

Nyla reached out for her coffee and the others followed suit.

He tried to reassure them. 'Listen, it's better to have some idea ... just in case.'

It didn't work. Their apathetic faces demonstrated their indifference.

'What are you saying, Harry?' asked Ben.

'All I'm trying to do is get you prepared. Nothing more ...' He looked at each of them in turn and they succumbed with a reluctant lowering of their heads. Harry smiled to himself and continued in a much lighter tone. 'If you get in a car or taxi, make sure you sit in the *back* seat on the opposite side to the driver ... then you can see him and watch what he's doing.'

They collectively nodded.

'If any of you are walking alone at night and feel you're being followed.'

They pulled back nervously.

Harry smiled and continued. 'Listen it may never happen. But it might. OK?'

They nodded.

He coughed and continued. 'Cross the road,' he said, firmly. 'Walk fast but don't run.' He raised his right hand and pointed into the distance. 'Take your time.'

He waited for their reaction.

They were still looking into the distance.

He coughed and continued. 'To check if they are following you, cross the road again and ...' He paused. 'If you are being followed ...' He looked at each of them in turn. 'This is very important. Shout "fire," as loud as you can ... and just keep repeating it.' He grinned. 'Most times, any potential mugger, or attacker will run away because, within seconds, someone will look out of a window to see what the hell is going on.' They all nodded their understanding. 'Also, walk close to the buildings, away from the kerb.'

They shot him a blank look.

'If a car pulls up to the kerb it is easy for them to grab you. Right?'

Nyla shuddered as she remembered the kidnap.

Harry reached out and squeezed her arm.

She smiled at him as she slowly relaxed.

'So keep close to the buildings. Understood?'

As he watched them visibly relax, he finished his coffee but kept the cup in his hand while he spoke. 'There are CCTV cameras on many of the main roads and busy streets.' He paused. 'Again, if you are being followed, keep an eye out for the nearest camera, look up to it and cross your arms.' He placed his cup in the saucer and demonstrated to them.

Without prompting they all followed suit.

'And you will see the camera tilt, acknowledging you. Once they've seen you, keep to the main road and they will monitor you and if necessary send out a police car.'

He looked at the girls. 'Keep your keys, purse, and phone in your pockets – *not* in your handbag.'

They tilted their heads and waited.

He spoke directly to Ben. 'Wallet, OK?'

Ben mumbled his response.

'And don't hang your handbag around your neck because, if someone wants it, they will yank it and it could do serious damage to your neck. Right?'

The girls silently questioned him.

He pointed at each of them to emphasise his concern. 'Listen, if they want it, let them have it.' He exhaled. 'It's easier to replace a bag than have your neck damaged.'

They looked at him and reluctantly they all mumbled their agreement.

He lit a cigarette. 'Lastly, programme the emergency number on speed dial on your mobile.' He smiled. 'If it's in your pocket, it's easy to reach and use.'

They smiled at him but were distracted by the sound of the high revving police car. They turned as it pulled up close to the tables, something the driver was either told to do or did of his own volition.

They took the opportunity to get up from the table and talked excitedly amongst themselves as they went back to work.

While Harry rearranged the chairs he watched as Zavos left his driver in the car and took his time to walk towards him.

'Morning, Harry, what is so urgent?' he asked, with a flourish of his gloved hand.

Harry motioned to him to join him on his boat.

Harry finished his cigarette before offering Zavos one

from his packet and slipping one into his own mouth. He lit both of them. He called out to Nyla and she appeared a few minutes later with a tray of coffee and four pies; two of each, "tyropita" – savoury cheese pie and "spanakopita" – spinach pie.

Zavos grabbed the nearest pie before Nyla had time to put down the tray and immediately chomped into it. 'Well, Harry.' He smiled and spoke with his mouth full. 'I must say this is very nice.' As he was about to take a second bite he stopped to study the inside of the pie. 'Very nice,' he said. He took another huge bite. 'In fact...' He smiled broadly. 'It's delicious.' He paused and eyed the remaining pies on the tray. 'But what is this all about, Harry? Is it a pie tasting?'

Harry shook his head and then nodded towards the tray of pies. 'Finish that and I'll show you.'

'I'm intrigued,' said Zavos, as he finished his spinach pie, wiped his hands in the serviette, and then ogled the cheese pie.

Harry moved the tray out of the policeman's reach, pushed his mobile towards him and showed him the photos of the dead dog in his hot tub.

Zavos took a brief look and gave an indifferent shrug. Instead, as he continued to lick his lips, he made to stand. He turned and looked across at the bar. 'Harry.' He licked at his lips once more and briefly closed his eyes as he relived the wonderful flavours of Mama's pie. He made an attempt to put his arm around Harry's neck. Harry pulled away. Zavos forced a smile and continued. 'My friend, you have a very successful taverna here and ...' He continued to wipe his hands in the serviette. 'I know you have made many ... many.' He emphasised the second "many" and he changed tack, coughed nervously while he chose the rest of his words carefully. He took a number of huge drags on his cigarette before he continued. 'Some *people* ...' He looked around and lowered his voice. 'Are very jealous.'

Harry tapped his foot on the deck of his boat and fidgeted.

Zavos paused and locked eyes with Harry. 'And angry –'

'So what are you saying, Zavos?' He moved close to the policeman. 'What they did was *criminal* ... and you know it.'

Zavos agreed with a nod. 'Hmm. Yes, I believe it was.'

Harry didn't like his response. He stood and deliberately rocked the boat. Zavos reached out and made a grab for the roof of the cabin. He succeeded and held on for dear life with both hands.

Harry, unaffected by the motion, continued. 'Are you suggesting that I run my bar into the ground? Just to please those fat ... lazy ... bastards?'

Zavos turned pale and continued to tremble as he scrambled onto the breakwater. He steadied himself, tugged at his jacket and turned. 'No, Harry ... live and let live, eh? They all deserve to make a living,' he said, with a sneer.

Harry moved aggressively towards the policeman. 'You must be fucking joking! There is no way that will happen again. If you won't do anything, then I ... *will*.'

Zavos walked unsteadily towards his car and turned. 'Be careful, Harry. No one is above the law ... and remember.' He stabbed his forefinger pointedly at Harry. 'We were here a long time before you ... you *English* arrived.'

Zavos loosened his tie, undid his shirt collar and motioned to his driver to leave.

*   *   *

116

Not to be defeated, Harry decided to sleep on his boat for the next few nights. He took his time to methodically rearrange the tables and chairs on the breakwater, close enough together so that whoever wanted to pass would have to move them. On the third night, which was dark and overcast, he heard footsteps and whispering on the breakwater. While the perpetrators were moving the chairs, Harry pounced. He threw an old fishing net over their heads. They punched the air as they made a futile attempt to escape. Harry dragged them towards him. He flicked the lid off the canister of car touch-up paint and indiscriminately sprayed their heads and arms, bright red. He drew them closer to him and snarled at them in Greek. 'Listen – you bastards. If you dare to do anything like this again … I will come and *find* you.' He snarled at them. 'And it won't be just a swim next time. Understand?'

They nodded frenetically and were still mumbling their incoherent reply when he pushed them into the sea, where they fought violently to escape the net, before swimming to shore.

The following morning, Harry sat on his boat anxiously flipping his mobile in his hand and reflecting on what his enemies might decide to try next.

Nyla joined him. 'Is it that bad, Dad?'

Harry nodded. 'Yeah.'

She frowned.

'It is and I'm worried about Nooda and Haya – they could get hurt if it turns nasty.'

'What about me?'

'I can look after you and Ben if you do as I say.' He paused. 'But the girls – I just can't.'

'So what are you going to do? You can't just throw them out on the streets –'

'Do you honestly think I would do that?'

Nyla blushed with embarrassment and spoke softly. 'Sorry, Dad. Course not.'

Harry cuddled her close. 'Listen, I've spoken to Zavos.' He looked at his mobile and slid it into his waistcoat pocket. 'And he said he can help them –'

'Him? Help?' She trembled. 'Do you really believe that?'

'Yeah. Zavos has suggested we talk to Savina and Yanis at the Harbour Side taverna.'

'OK.' She looked towards the taverna on the quay and then back to Harry. 'Can I tell them?'

He smiled at her. 'Course you can. Go on.'

She stood and rushed into the bar.

Although he had never been in the taverna Harry knew the owners by sight. Savina and her husband Yanis were Greek Cypriots, in their mid-forties, who had been running the successful Harbour Side taverna since they took it over from Savina's parents. Working seven days a week, they had both let themselves go, and were now well overweight. Their bar still retained a steady flow of regular business from local people when the tourists left at the end of the summer so they chose to remain open throughout the winter months.

Harry, Nyla, Nooda, and Haya visited the taverna and while Harry sat in the bar with Yanis and drank coffee, Savina showed the three girls the luxury first floor flat that was to be their accommodation. Nooda and Haya sat on the balcony at the intricately carved olive wood table with matching chairs.

They pinched themselves as they gazed out at the idyllic view across the harbour and, in the distance, Harry's Bar.

Savina poured the tea and they excitedly discussed the arrangements. Nooda and Haya were overawed at their good fortune and agreed to start work the next day.

A few hours later, Nyla dragged her feet up the stairs as she followed the girls, who were carrying their meagre belongings.

'Don't be sad. We can still see each other, Nyla,' said Nooda, pointing at Harry's Bar at the end of the breakwater.

'Yes, and we can go out on our days off,' spurted Haya enthusiastically.

Nyla forced a smile. 'I know,' she said, sadly.

Two weeks passed and neither of the girls had contacted Nyla or Harry. 'I'm going to the taverna in the morning, Dad,' said Nyla. She shuffled on the spot and fiddled with her mobile phone. 'Why haven't they contacted me?'

'Give them time, they have a lot to learn and don't forget … they're being paid to work now, so things will be very different.'

Nyla accepted her father's reasoning with a reluctant shrug.

Another two weeks passed and Nyla visited the Harbour Side taverna on her day off.

Savina told her that both of the girls were shopping with her husband and would be back later unless of course they asked to explore the island with him.

'Can you ask one of them to give me a call,' asked Nyla.

Savina smiled. 'Of course, I will. They have been busy.' In a split second her manner changed and her smile was replaced with a grimace. 'They still have a lot to learn, you know.'

Harry was cleaning the coffee machine when Nyla returned. 'Are you alright, love?'

'No, I'm not,' she said, angrily.

'What's so bad that your world has crashed?'

'I went to see Nooda and Haya this afternoon –'

'Yeah ... and?'

'They weren't there. SHE said they were out shopping.' She screwed up her face. 'But I don't believe her.'

'Alright,' he said, 'let's give it a few more days and we'll both go across.'

She shot him a mystified look.

'Yes?' He grinned at her. 'Course I'll come with you.'

She smiled the widest of smiles and hugged him. 'Thanks, Dad.'

When Harry and Nyla visited the Harbour Side taverna, Savina was wiping down the tables and Yanis was prepping food for the evening. They both appeared shocked to see Harry and Nyla standing in their taverna.

Nyla walked up to Savina before she spoke. 'You promised you would ask Nooda and Haya to call me. But they haven't,' she said, firmly.

Savina screwed up his face. 'Erm ...'

Harry stepped forward. 'We want to see them. Now,' he demanded.

Savina shook her head and gave him an abhorrent grin. 'You'll be lucky,' she said.

'What are you talking about?'

Yanis moved towards Harry. 'They ran away?' he said, coolly.

Nyla pushed past Harry and pummelled the Greek's fat hairy chest.

Yanis reached out and grabbed her wrists.

'Get your hands off her – now!' roared Harry.

Yanis didn't flinch.

Harry stepped forward and smacked him across the head with his open hands.

The Greek Cypriot released Nyla and made an issue of feigning serious injury by moaning and pressing his hands tight against his head.

Harry exhaled some of his anger. 'Don't fuck with me. I'll ask you again – where are they?'

Savina screamed at Harry. 'We've already told you. The ungrateful bastards have run away,' she said, foaming at the mouth.

Yanis, still rubbing his ears and undeterred, shouted at Harry. 'Useless pieces of shit – I don't know why we listened to you.'

Savina raised her hands and pointed towards the phone. 'If you don't get out of here, we'll call the police.'

Harry let out a menacing groan but knew he would not get any more answers and made to move towards the door.

Nyla tugged at his arms and pleaded with him. 'We can't just go.' She shook with a combination of anguish and anger as she continued. 'Come on, tell me.' She pounded at his chest. 'Why would they run away?'

Harry grabbed her flaying arms and eased her gently towards the door. He didn't speak until they were outside, and far enough away from the bar for Yanis and Savina to be able to hear him. He guided her to an empty bench on the edge of the harbour wall. 'Come on, sit down,' he said, quietly.

She initially refused by shrugging her shoulders and stomping up and down the quayside. She eventually calmed down and sat beside him.

Harry pulled her towards him and placed his arm around her. 'Sorry, love. I'll have a word with Zavos.' He stroked her long hair and pulled it over her shoulder. 'He may know something.'

'It's my fault, Dad –'

'It's not your fault.'

She pulled away from him.

Harry continued. 'Don't even say that.' He moved to hug her. She edged further away. Harry continued in a low voice. 'I know it's hard –'

'Hard?' She shook her head. 'Where are they now? Where would they go? Surely they would have told me.'

Harry spoke in almost a whisper. 'I don't want to be cruel love, but they're not used to living like this.'

'Like what?'

'Look. I've been to Aleppo.' He remembered the tension and uncertainty of the inhabitants who had expected to die overnight but the following morning found they were still alive to suffer the hell for yet another long day. He continued. 'Strangely they are used to struggling and I reckon they felt odd. It has affected them here –'

'Affected them? How can you say that?' She sobbed out of control. 'They loved it with me.' She paused and looked at him sympathetically. 'No ... I meant with us.'

Harry reached out for her hand and this time she let him take it. He squeezed it. 'Listen, sometimes it takes a long time for people to adjust to a safe place. It's too much for them to take in – when they have somewhere safe to live – away from the threats.'

She screwed up her face and her eyes narrowed.

Harry continued. 'Julian told me that when he finished renovating a block of flats in Birmingham he found a young woman sleeping rough in the builder's shed, at the back of the block.'

'Yeah?'

'Well … he had a tiny store area on the ground floor of the flats and had his builders convert it into a bedsit. He furnished it with second-hand furniture and put in everything anyone would need,' he smiled, 'even a television.' He took a deep breath. 'Not a new one … but still a flat screen.' He squeezed Nyla's hand once more and continued. 'She moved in.' His manner changed and he rubbed his chin. 'Julian went back one morning to see how she was settling in before he flew back here.'

Nyla smiled positively.

Harry sighed. 'Do you know what?'

'What?' she asked expectantly.

He raised his voice. 'She was sleeping in the flats – on the first floor landing.' He punched the air. 'In a cardboard box –'

'No way –'

'She was,' said Harry vehemently. 'She'd never slept in her bed in her bedsit.'

'Why on earth not?'

'You won't believe this –'

'Try me.'

'She told Julian she didn't feel safe.'

'What?'

'She said, she actually felt safer – sleeping rough – on the floor.' He sighed. 'On the landing.'

'Why?'

'She said she could hear anyone coming up the stairs and could protect herself.'

Nyla looked at him open mouthed. 'She could lock the flat door.'

'Course she could, but she wasn't used to being locked in and she felt trapped.'

Nyla was gobsmacked.

'Now do you understand why the girls have run off? Especially, when you consider what they went through and … where they came from.' This time Harry made a concerted effort and pulled Nyla towards him. 'I *will* call, Zavos.' He squeezed her tight. 'Give me time, OK?'

She rubbed violently at her eyes and looked up at him. 'OK.'

Harry's call to Zavos resulted in the inspector's usual response. 'If I hear anything, I'll let you know, my friend.'

For the next few days, Nyla was inconsolable and spent much of the time in her room or with Mama.

Out of the blue, she received a text from Nooda.

> **Please help us.**
> **Nooda and Haya**
> **xx**

An hour later, Yanis and Savina visited Harry's Bar. 'What have you done with them? Where are they?' demanded Yanis.

'You told me they had run away,' said Nyla.

'That's right,' said Harry.

'They did,' said Yanis.

He looked at Savina.

She said, 'But when they realised they couldn't leave the island –'

'They got here without them,' said Harry.

She snapped at him. 'That was different –'

'Sure it was,' he said, as he reflected upon the fateful events around their arrival.

Savina continued. 'They came back.'

Yanis forced a laugh. 'Yeah, they came back alright.'

Harry and Nyla nodded their agreement. 'So?'

'They've disappeared again,' said Savina.

Yanis shot them a forceful look. 'If you see them, be sure to let us know. OK?'

'Sure,' said Harry. But his body language said otherwise. He waited until they had driven off and he sat down and motioned for Nyla to join him.

'They're lying.'

'Even I know that,' said Nyla. 'They both had passports didn't they?'

'Yeah, they did but have they still got them? Maybe those slimy bas ...' He coughed. 'People ... or whatever you want to call them ... had them.' Harry swallowed hard. 'So where the hell are they now?'

'I don't know,' replied Nyla. She paused. 'A silly question ...' She took a deep breath. 'But could they get off the island without passports?'

'Unlikely now,' he said, 'things are much tougher with the refugees and migrants arriving every day. Maybe that's why they came back – to get them.'

She smiled. 'Yeah, if they left in a hurry the first time ...

maybe they couldn't get them from where they'd hidden them.'

'Well, there you go.' Harry motioned to her for a coffee.

She crossed her arms, pushed herself deep into the chair, and scowled at him across the table.

He nodded and sighed. 'OK. I'll have a word with Zavos.' He waited patiently for her reaction.

There was none.

Harry asked once more. 'OK?'

Her mood slowly changed and she pushed herself to her feet. 'Coffee it is, sir.'

Harry called Zavos, who replied in his standard matter of fact way. He told Harry that he would ask his officers to keep an eye out for them and leave their details at the airport. Apart from that, there was little else he could do

CHAPTER FOURTEEN

I Will Survive

Ben was playing the piano, surrounded by a group of holiday makers who were singing along with the tunes, when he suddenly collapsed and slumped to the floor, unconscious. Harry called an ambulance, rushed to perform CPR on him, and laid him on his side in the recovery position. The paramedics arrived within ten minutes and after carrying out emergency treatment they stretchered him to the ambulance. With blue lights and siren blasting, they raced to Paphos General Hospital. The four storey pyramid shaped hospital, built in 1992, was long considered to be one of the best hospitals in the Middle East but it was now in decline and was unable to handle the rapidly growing population of Paphos.

While Ben lay in a coma the duty doctor walked into the room and, after checking the myriad of machines and his records, he looked directly at Harry. 'I must tell the police about this ...' He checked his clipboard. 'Mr Clark.' He lowered his eyes. 'It's very serious. With these bad drugs, people will die –'

'What?'

'We will save him if we can –'

'Save him?'

'Yes it is a very bad drug.' While he looked down at Ben he stroked his short sculptured beard and continued. 'Yes,' he tutted, 'very bad.'

Harry and Nyla sat beside Ben's bed and waited in silence, except for the incessant bleeping of the lifesaving machines.

An hour later Zavos, flanked by two uniformed policeman, stomped into ITU and made for Harry and Nyla. He didn't speak but, after looking down at Ben and across to the life-saving equipment, he turned to Harry. 'It is a pity, my friend but these dangerous drugs were taken in your bar –'

'What the hell is that supposed to mean, Zavos?'

'It is simple. That young man works for you at your bar and ...' He pointed at Ben. 'Look at him. He could die –'

Nyla screamed out. 'He's not going to die ... is he, Dad?' Harry made a pathetic attempt to shake his head but it was unconvincing. 'He won't, will he?' screamed Nyla.

Harry patted her shoulder and sighed as his anger boiled over. 'Nah. He'll be fine,' he said half-heartedly.

Zavos ignored Harry's comment with a loud huff and the flicking of his shoulders. He tilted his head back and took his time to look down at Ben. 'I must close your bar, Harry –'

'What?'

Harry stood and moved close to Zavos and pushed his face into his.

The policemen at the door reached for their holsters and moved towards Harry.

Zavos raised his arms, motioned to them to pull back, and trembled as he struggled to speak. 'Alright, Harry. You may stay open until we find out who is selling these drugs,' he said nervously.

Harry looked down at Ben. 'That was slipped into the kid's drink.' He paused and glared at Zavos. 'And you fucking know it.' He stared hard at Zavos and waited for his agreement.

Nothing.

Harry continued. 'You know I would never allow that in my place. You know too well it's everywhere on the island and you do fuck all about it.' He glared at Zavos. 'Do you?'

He muttered his response. 'We try, Harry.'

Harry wouldn't let go and continued in a raised voice. 'Really? What about the Russians – they control you ... and everything else – right?'

Zavos looked to his men and asked them to move back. He turned to face Harry and exhaled his incoherent reply.

Harry extended his arms as far as he could, raised his hands in the air, and outstretched his fingers. 'You know, Zavos.' He took a deep breath. 'You have a very short memory.'

Zavos looked at him vacantly.

'The dead dog – in my fucking hot tub?'

Zavos nodded. 'Ah, yes.'

'You know *your* people want me to fail,' said Harry. He stamped his feet. 'Fuck you.' He made to move towards the policemen at the door. They stiffened and once again reached for their holsters. He stopped a few feet from them. 'Fuck you all,' he screamed, as he returned to his seat next to the bed.

Zavos threw up his hands. 'Harry, what do expect me to do?' He fiddled with his gloves and forced a grin. 'I agree with you my friend, but there is too much around. Do you expect me to arrest every tourist on the island?'

Harry glared at him. 'Course, I do. And the Russian dealers,' he snarled.

Zavos ignored his remark and continued. 'I will be lynched by the hotelkeepers and tour operators and ...' He didn't finish his sentence. Instead he paused and shook his head.

'And the Russians?' asked Harry. He sneered. 'They'll probably kill you, right?'

Zavos ignored him once more and continued. 'And, what the hell the tourist board would do to us doesn't bear thinking about.'

Harry shrugged his shoulders. 'And?'

There was no reaction.

Zavos sucked in air and took his time to exhale. 'OK, my friend. Maybe you can deal with this yourself but if we have any more events like this – we will shut you down.' He raised his voice. 'For good.' He tapped his glove on his bare hand. 'You understand what I'm saying, Harry?'

Harry closed his eyes and wrung his hands. 'I see, Zavos.' Harry opened his eyes and continued. 'So once again, I'm on my own?'

'Do it Harry ... but don't go too far,' he said, in little more than a whisper.

Ben came out of the coma a few days later and had no recollection of who had slipped the drug into his beer bottle. After a short rest he was back working and playing at the bar as normal.

As a deterrent to any potential drug users, Harry installed mock CCTV cameras around the bar and installed blue fluorescent light tubes in the toilets.

CHAPTER FIFTEEN

All Shook Up

Harry clicked off his mobile, walked to his boat, and dialled a number. 'Hello, Nichole, do you fancy lunch next Monday?'

She laughed. 'Really? And what have I done to deserve the honour?' She paused. 'Ah. I get it. You want me to do that feature on your place, right?'

Harry smiled into the mobile. 'We'll talk about it next Monday. Come about two and I'll get Mama to put a picnic together.'

'See you then,' she said, excitedly.

Nichole arrived a few minutes early and Harry was already in his boat – tidying up. She parked her Saab and joined him. She looked breathtaking in a flowing patterned blouse of tropical flowers, hibiscus, orchids, alpinia and amazon lilies, hip hugging red shorts and red patent sandals.

Harry helped her onto the boat and gave her a gentle hug before sitting her down. 'Sit back and relax and we'll have lunch in about half an hour. OK?'

She smiled at him. 'Whatever you wish, Captain,' she said, with a flourish of her right hand.

Harry made his way slowly out to sea and followed the coast towards Chlorakas beach. He slowed and tied the boat to a fisherman's marker buoy and turned off the engine. He switched on his CD player and, while soft summer sounds floated out of the speakers, he placed a tablecloth on one of the seats. While Nichole laid out the food, he took a bottle of Biblia Chora Ovilos Semillion Assyrtiko 2014 from the cold box, and uncorked it using the corkscrew in his Swiss knife. As he flicked it open he recalled the last time it was used, many months earlier, for violent means, in the warehouse.

Nichole smiled when she saw the wine label. 'Wow. Can I say you are certainly "pushing the boat out" today?' She giggled. 'This must be important.'

He poured two glasses and passed one to her.

They both raised their glasses in the air and clinked them together. 'Gia mas,' they both said, with a flourish.

Harry sipped at his wine while Nichole picked her way through the kritharaki me pastouma – spicy sausage – served with grated halloumi cheese, and the chicken souvlaki wrap that Mama had so lovingly prepared. After eating more than half of the food, Nichole stretched out on the deck to relax and enjoy the sun.

Harry opened a second bottle of the expensively delicious wine, poured two glasses and then served the dessert of Kateifi with ice-cream and nuts.

'That was fantastic,' said Nichole.

Harry smiled and licked his lips. 'Mama can certainly cook.'

Nichole showed her impatience by slipping off her sandals

and wiggling her toes in the air. 'Come on, Harry, I've been very patient and waited long enough,' she said, sensually.

He nodded his head thoughtfully.

'What is this all about?' she asked.

Harry took his time to refill her glass.

She smiled at him apprehensively. 'What is so important that you want me to be drunk before you tell me?'

He took a sip of his wine and nervously strangled a cough. 'Well ... you may be disappointed.' He shrugged his shoulders. 'I don't know.'

'Try me, Harry,' she teased.

Harry pulled out his mobile and flicked to the photos of the dog carcass in the hot tub. She pulled back and urged. He opened a bottle of water and passed it to her. 'Are you, OK?' he asked.

She swallowed most of the water before looking at him. 'Is that for real?'

Harry nodded.

Nichole was pale and badly shaken. 'Where was that?' she spluttered.

Harry sucked at his top lip. 'The hot tub ... at the bar ... recently.'

'Did you tell Zavos?'

'Course I did.'

'And?'

'What you would expect? Fuck all.' He smiled at her. 'But I caught the bastards.' He reflected and smirked back at her. 'They won't try that again.'

'How can you be so sure?'

He sniggered. 'Let's just say, I know.'

Nichole reached for her wine glass.

It was empty.

Harry refilled it and waited until she drank most of it. He topped it up and spoke while he refilled his glass. 'What do you know about the bent police and the bribes they're taking from bar owners across the island based on so-called noise pollution?'

'You mean the local bar owners are blaming the British and Irish bars for taking their business?'

'Too right they are,' he said. 'Several have paid bent lawyers who did nothing ... fuck all ... except take their money.' He sighed. 'The bastards.'

She looked concerned. 'Are they into you too?'

'The police have been along a few times, conveniently when Zavos is not there, and they have warned not only us but other bars to turn down the volume, or ...' He paused and changed his tone. 'They said they would close us down. But last night there was no sign of the "official" police.' He offered Nichole a cigarette and although she didn't smoke she took one. Harry lit it and continued. 'Do you know the bastards have even come complaining about the noise when Ben was playing the piano? Can you believe that – a fucking piano?'

She tilted her head and nodded. 'Um,' she said, looking concerned. She emptied her glass and Harry refilled it once more.

'I've spoken to the owners at a few of the other bars and one of them had the bastards turn up before the band even started playing.' He huffed. 'Not even a note.'

Nichole bit her lip and turned her face away from the sun.

Harry continued. 'Last night they took the speakers from the bar, and the entire band's gear ... guitars, drums, amplifiers – everything.'

'Surely you would have had something to say about that?'

'Ah, ah.' He sniggered. 'That's the point – I wasn't there.'

She laughed loudly. 'But you're always there, Harry. You're almost part of the furniture.'

'Not last night.' Harry shook his head violently. 'It's like they knew. We ran out of beer so I had to go into town and pick up more.' He sighed. 'Ben was grabbed by a group of heavies; men, who I know for *sure,* were police, out of uniform –'

'Is he alright?'

Harry grinned. 'They didn't hurt him. They held him and got the band to stand aside while they took their equipment and loaded it into an unmarked white van.' He swore under his breath. 'Their excuse was that their music was too loud.' He huffed. 'That's nonsense. What happens is ...' He took a huge drag on his cigarette. 'The local bars call the police and, to cover themselves, turn down their music before the bastards arrive.' He threw his head back in frustration. 'You've lived here long enough to know it's going on?'

She nodded. 'Yeah, but I didn't realise there was so much of it.'

'Some bar owners have paid them ...' He exhaled loudly and shook his head. 'To leave their places alone –'

'You're not paying them are you?'

'What do you think? 'I'll shoot them if I have too.'

'Really?'

'Too right .... I will,' he said, indignantly.

She looked shocked. 'You can't do that,' she said. 'Why not call the British Embassy and ask them to help you all?'

'I already have and they gave me the names of lawyers who they said *may* be able to help.'

She looked positive.

He sniggered. 'Do you know how many?'

She shook her head.

'Thirty five.' He forced a laugh. 'Can you believe it?'

She took a lengthy drag on her cigarette, exhaled the smoke, and looked at him in total disbelief. She mouthed the number back to him.

'Yeah ... that's right, thirty five. And most of them are fucking bent as hell.'

'Are you sure, Harry?'

'Oh yeah,' he said, confidently. He took a deep breath. 'So, my reason for our lunch is to see if you will cover the story.' He looked directly at her. 'And I mean cover, *not* cover-up.'

She smiled back at him.

'Harry you are full of surprises. I thought you had an ulterior motive ... you know.' She grinned. 'Something else,' she said, as she licked her lips seductively.

Harry didn't reply to her question. Instead, he stood, and refilled her glass with the last of the wine, then began to repack the picnic basket.

'OK, Harry. I understand. But if you ever ...' she intimated sensually.

He knew exactly what she meant. He smiled at her and, as he lowered his head he nodded knowingly. 'Oh, I forgot to tell you. I'll be on Sunshine Radio and Rock FM tomorrow talking about this shit.' He exhaled angrily. 'I'm not afraid of these bastards.' He smashed the lid of the basket down, pushed the pin through it brutally as though it was one of the attackers, and slid it along the deck. 'They won't beat me.'

Nichole briefly felt intimidated. 'I'll run the story but you need to be careful, Harry. If the police are involved they won't want you to mess up their moneymaking scheme, will they?'

Harry mumbled his reply.

*   *   *

Harry sat in the studio with the huge microphone a few inches from his nose and waited nervously for Simon, the radio station DJ, to introduce him.

The Bob Marley song finished.

Simon's listeners loved reggae.

'Well, this morning I have a very special guest.' He faded up the music and then down again. 'If any of you haven't had the good fortune of visiting Harry's Bar at the end of the breakwater, you should.' He paused. 'I love it.' His voice had a genuine delight in it. 'Well I'm lucky enough to have Harry, yes, *that* Harry, here in the studio with me.' He smiled at his guest. 'Hello, Harry, welcome.'

'Morning, Simon,' said Harry, nervously.

'So, Harry, tell the listeners. How long have you been here on the island?'

Harry stifled a cough and cleared his throat. 'I was here twenty years ago, in the army.'

'Ah.'

'But three years ago I came back and asked if I could lease the building at the end of the breakwater.'

'Three years?'

'Yeah. Did you see what it was like then?'

'Yes, I did, Harry. So?'

Harry grunted and was about to speak.

Simon interrupted him. 'Wow, Harry. Correct me if I'm wrong you've only been open since April. Is that right?'

'Yeah, we have.' Harry smiled proudly at Simon. 'I wanted to do the work myself and have something that not only I could be proud of.' He paused and smiled again. 'But somewhere people would want to visit. Local people, as well as the tourists.'

'You've certainly done that alright. It's always busy.' He laughed. 'And I love the hot tub.'

'Erm, yes,' said Harry. 'It's very popular … especially late at night.' He paused. 'But now we've had to charge a deposit on the towels. So many were stolen for souvenirs, we couldn't go on losing them. It was costing me a fortune.'

Simon laughed. 'Can they bring their own?'

'Of course, they can,' said Harry. 'But they don't.'

Simon nodded. 'OK. So, on a more serious note, Harry, what is going on with the English and Irish bars?'

Harry took a deep breath. 'Well … we are all getting pressure put on us to stop the live music.' He forced a laugh. 'People are saying it's too loud.' He raised his voice. 'Louder than the local bars –'

'Really?'

'Yeah, I know it's crazy.' Harry clenched his fists under the table. 'And, more to the point.' He sighed. 'It's total nonsense.'

Simon sounded genuinely concerned. 'Who is saying that, Harry?' He paused before he finished the sentence. 'The police?'

Harry sniggered. 'On the face of it, it isn't. But we all know different –'

'That's serious, Harry.'

Harry continued. 'You have to remember, Simon … it's only the English and Irish bars they are targeting.'

'Why?'

Harry beamed. 'It's simple, we are doing the better business.' He paused. 'And the locals want it.'

He watched Simon and waited for a response.

There was none.

Harry continued. 'Look, it's like this. If we don't pay

whoever they are.' He paused for effect. 'You either get shut down or the band's equipment gets taken away.' He coughed. 'In effect – they steal it.'

'But who is doing it?'

Harry sniggered. 'I can't say on air –'

'No, no, of course not,' said Simon hastily. He shot his guest a concerned look, hoping his reply dealt with Harry's comment. 'But you know who it is?'

'Yes, of course.' Harry laughed. 'They hide in plain sight … in ordinary clothes but –'

'Wow.' Simon was visibly shocked. 'So what are you saying, Harry?'

'I can't say anymore … but what I will say. It has to *stop*.' The listeners could hear the anger and at the same time frustration in Harry's voice.

Simon pulled it back with a smile. 'OK, Harry, time for some more music.' He faded in some non-descript background music. 'Keep me posted. Will you come back on and update me and the listeners?'

'Of course, I will.'

'Thanks, Harry.' As he faded up the music he spoke over it. 'Well listeners, that was Harry Clark from Harry's Bar … you must check out the place. You won't be disappointed.'

Simon pushed up the faders and *Black*, an out and out rock track, by the English, ex-pat band, Dynamite, blasted out of the studio speakers.

They shook hands. 'Don't forget, Harry, let me know what happens.' Simon looked Harry in the eye. 'I hope you can sort it out and … and don't forget to keep me posted. Will you?' he said.

Harry nodded. 'Yeah. I will.'

*   *   *

After several telephone calls and emails to the British Embassy, they reluctantly gave Harry the name of a reliable and trustworthy lawyer. True to her word, Karina Christopholous presented her application and, much to everyone's surprise except her own, she obtained a Court Order the same day.

Harry called Nichole.

'I know, Harry. You got a Court Order,' she said. 'News travels fast, especially if the police are involved in anything underhand.'

'It didn't before, did it?'

'I know, Harry. But they did manage to keep it covered up until now.' She laughed loudly. 'Remember, you had my help too.'

'Yeah, agreed.' He smirked to himself. 'Along with the radio interviews,' he said.

Nichole continued. 'I know that, but the police department can only allow so much shit to go on before they have to do something about it and clean up their act.' She whistled. 'It was a great campaign, Harry.'

Harry grunted.

'Can I arrange for a photographer to go with you and the band when you collect their equipment?'

'Sure you can.' He paused. 'But no pictures of me, right?'

'Sure, Harry. I understand.' She flicked her fingers and thought to herself. 'So what is it with having your picture in the paper?'

Harry killed the call.

When the musicians walked into the basement where their equipment had been stored, they couldn't believe what they saw. It was stacked with musical instruments and equipment taken illegally from musicians over the past few years.

Nichole's first article and the follow up front page, with photographs of the band members standing in front of the stockpile of instruments and equipment, sent shockwaves through the police in Paphos and surrounding towns. Within days many of those "police" were redeployed to Limassol and Nicosia.

The police car parked at the end of the breakwater and while the driver sat and waited, Zavos walked slow and tenaciously towards Harry's Bar. He had a wry smile on his face as he walked inside. He grabbed a bar stool and sat down. He took his time to remove his mirrored sunglasses, symbolically cleaned them, and then placed them neatly on the bar in front of him. 'Well, Harry you have certainly caused a lot of upset around the island this time,' he said, vindictively.

Harry grunted and slid the Inspector a coffee and a glass of Metaxa. 'Do you know I've had anonymous calls threatening me and the bar?' he said.

He waited for a reaction from Zavos.

Zavos grimaced.

Harry grinned at Zavos and stiffened his arms. Keeping his large hands on the edge of the bar, he straightened his back and stretched his whole body. 'But they should have known better. Come on Zavos you knew that shite wouldn't work with me?' Harry lit a cigarette. 'It had to be done and ...' He smiled at Zavos. 'I did it without needing to kill anybody.'

Zavos drank the brandy in one gulp and then sipped at his coffee. 'Agreed, my friend ... but be careful.'

CHAPTER SIXTEEN

Time Is On My Side

The phone in Harry's Bar rang. He reached for it and spoke. 'Good morning, Harry's Bar.'

'It was you who did this to us,' said the female caller.

'Who is it?'

She cried as she spoke. 'You know who it is.'

'Is that you Nooda?'

'It's Haya –'

'Where are you? I can help you.'

'You said that before. You are a bastard. It is your fault. We were forced to work for those vile and filthy people.'

Harry was lost for words and stuttered his nonsensical reply.

She continued. 'It doesn't matter where we are – we are safe.' Haya broke down as she trembled with a combination of anger and fear. 'You won't get away with it. Wherever you go – for sure – we will find you.'

Nooda took the phone. 'And we will have our revenge.'

The line went dead.

Harry took a deep breath, walked along the breakwater,

and lit a cigarette. He finished it and lit another one before sitting down at a table well away from the bar, and tried to take in what he'd just heard.

Yanis and Savina drove up the breakwater and parked as close as they could to the entrance to Harry's bar, blocking access to many of the tables and chairs.

Harry was drying glasses and restocking the bar when Yanis and Savina walked in and made straight for him.

Harry looked up and smiled. 'To what do I owe the pleasure,' he said.

They scowled at him.

'What the hell did you do with them?' asked Yanis.

'What?'

'Where are they?' asked Savina.

'They called me ...' said Harry.

'What did they say?' said Yanis.

'Don't plead ignorance. You both know what happened and I can't blame them for getting the hell out of it,' said Harry.

'They are lying, ungrateful bastards,' said Yanis. 'They don't appreciate what we did for them.'

Harry grinned at them mindlessly and attempted to swallow his anger.

It failed.

'If they're not here then you won't mind us looking around. Will you?' said Yanis, forebodingly.

Harry closed his eyes and took a deep breath before he reopened them. 'Get out of my sight. Now!' Harry raised his hands in the air and as he lowered them he stretched his arms and took his time to point a forefinger at each of them menacingly. 'Before I do something ...' He exhaled. '... I'll regret.' He gritted his teeth, glared at them, and clenched his fists. 'Fuck off – both of you.'

They fell back and walked a few paces towards the door.

Savina turned. 'You will regret what you've done. Wait and see.'

Harry muttered under his breath, shook his head, and stomped off towards the kitchen.

Harry told Nyla that Savina and Yanis had come to the bar looking for the girls. She broke down and shook her head wildly as she mumbled through her tears. 'That is so sad. It's terrible. Where are they?'

Harry looked at her compassionately as even he tried to come to terms with what he'd heard.

Nyla looked across to him. 'Where will they go now?'

Harry sighed deeply and shuddered. 'They told me they have their passports.'

Nyla forced a half smile. 'So they can go anywhere?'

'Only if they have money,' replied Harry.

'Yeah, you're right.'

'Maybe they'll call back.'

'If they do, can I talk to them, please?' begged Nyla.

Harry nodded. 'Sure.'

He knew that was very unlikely.

CHAPTER SEVENTEEN

All Cried Out

It was the close to end of the season, the tourist trade had all but fizzled out, and Harry, Ben and Nyla closed the bar early and were having a quiet meal at a restaurant on the quay. Nyla ordered for all of them: souvla, a popular Cyprus dish with large pieces of neck and shoulder of lamb, pork and chicken. The meat was cut on the bone into chunks about the size of a medium onion and slow cooked on a long skewer over a charcoal barbecue.

After months of wondering and waiting, Nyla felt the time was right to ask Harry about Stryker, his alter ego, and reluctantly he talked about it. 'I've done some bad things I regret and nor can I unsee the things I've seen.' He paused. 'It's with me for a lifetime. The things you can't change are in the past.'

Nyla felt sorry for him as she remembered what she'd seen in the warehouse.

Ben emptied his beer glass and looked along the quay and out towards the bar. He looked and looked again. 'Harry, is that smoke?'

Harry strained his eyes and watched. 'Fuck, yes it is. The

bar's on fire! Call the fire brigade – NOW!' he screamed. As he jumped up from his seat his chair crashed onto the floor.

He ran towards the bar but by the time he reached the breakwater the building was well alight. He entered the building as the blazing timbers crashed around him. The plastic tablecloths were already alight and melting onto the wooden tables and chairs.

'MAMA!' screamed Harry. He grabbed a bar cloth and doused it with water from the jug on the bar and held it against his mouth. He squinted as the smoke began to burn his eyes and fill his lungs.

He reached the kitchen.

He tried to open the door but it was blocked by burning chairs. He kicked out and the door crashed open. The kitchen was well ablaze and many of Mama's cooking ingredients including the flour, sugar, and powdered milk, which were normally harmless, exploded randomly around him. As the ceiling and walls came crashing down he gritted his teeth and swore under his breath. He had no option but to get out of the inferno. As he made his way blindly through the flames towards the exit, the first of the LPG gas bottles exploded in the kitchen and he was thrown against the bar. At the same time, the bottles of spirit on the wall behind the bar exploded, propelling shards of glass through the air. Harry stumbled blindly between the burning armchairs, settees, tables and chairs until he made it to relative safety on the breakwater.

The fire engines eventually arrived and raced along the harbourside, lights flashing, with their wailing sirens filling the air. They drove as near to the bar as they could but were only able to get to within fifty metres of the fire. They took what seemed an inordinate amount of time to set up their hoses before making a futile attempt to put out the fire. An aerial tower on one of the fire engines reached as far as it could, but it was useless as the water they sprayed fell well short of the flames. When the rest of the LPG bottles exploded and the remainder of the roof blew up into the air, the firemen immediately pulled back and waited. Harry's boat was then hit by the hot falling tiles and burning timber. Within minutes it was also on fire and began to sink.

Although the main fire was eventually extinguished, smoke continued to fill the night sky. Harry stood at the police cordon and scrutinised the building in disbelief. His hands and arms were burned, his face blackened by the smoke and his hair thick with debris. He was guided to an ambulance by a paramedic and after receiving emergency medical treatment he rejoined Ben and Nyla at the bar.

Nyla piled several spoons of sugar into a cup of tea and held the cup up to Harry's blistered lips. He sipped at it and trembled uncontrollably.

Yes, he'd lost the bar, but Mama was dead and it was his fault.

Ben and Nyla both had their thoughts but neither wanted to be the first to speak. They wiped at their tears and exhaled as the shock waves continued to sweep through their bodies.

'Fuck,' said Harry, with laboured breathing. He looked at Nyla. She forced a smile. He continued. 'Sorry, Nyla but Mama was in there.'

Nyla broke down and wept.

Ben wiped at his eyes while Harry edged his bandaged hand across his red-veined tearful eyes. They continued to sit in silence while they each took their time to recall their memories and thoughts of their dearest friend.

Harry exhaled loudly. 'I should have saved her.' He wiped at his eyes. 'It's my fault.' He choked and took his time to exhale. 'And now she's dead.'

Ben spoke, 'Harry, you can't blame yourself. You did all you could –'

'DID I?' screamed Harry. 'I should have been the one to have died. Not Mama.'

Nyla hugged him and as he released his guilt he let his head fall into her shoulder.

He lifted his head and spoke. 'I remember the first time I saw her.' He looked blindly ahead and remembered. 'She was working at a burger stand in the old town ... at three in the morning. Can you believe that?'

He sniffed.

Silence.

Harry continued. 'She was surrounded by drunken slobs and idiots yelling foul obscenities at her.' He sniffed and wiped at his nose with his bandaged hand. 'I told her to leave.'

Ben and Nyla looked at him and waited for him to continue.

'I got rid of the scum and told her she could come and work for me.' He forced a smile. 'It was the best thing I could have done.' He paused. 'Why should she have to take that crap night after night for a few euros an hour?' He rubbed at his tearful eyes and wiped at his nose. 'But look what I did – I killed her. SHE'S DEAD!'

A police car, with blue light flashing, pulled up at the restaurant. Zavos got out and took his time to walk towards them. When he reached their table his sombre face broke into a smile.

Ben and Nyla looked up at him expectantly but Harry, still traumatised, continued to hang his head low.

Zavos took his time to straighten his jacket and adjust his cap. He loved the attention. He faked a cough and smiled at each of them in turn, waiting until Harry lifted his head. 'You'll be pleased to know that Sofia Daukas is alive –'

'What?' asked Ben.

'Who?' asked Nyla.

Harry looked away, highlighting his lack of interest.

When he had their undivided attention Zavos continued. 'Harry, it's your cook.' He grinned. 'That's her name.' He frowned at Harry. 'I can't believe you didn't know that.'

'Why should we?' screamed Nyla. 'She's always been Mama to us.'

Zavos grunted and continued smugly. 'She was visiting her sick husband in Poli Crysochoussister – he's a fisherman.'

Nyla spoke. 'I didn't know she had a husband. She never mentioned him.'

'She has,' said Zavos. He grinned, exuding self-confidence. 'And … she will be coming on the next bus.' He turned to Harry and smirked. 'It's what we police do. Our job.'

Harry grunted his response. 'Hmm.'

Zavos chose to ignore him and while he smoked a whole cigarette he spent the time looking out towards the smouldering building. He flicked the cigarette butt away and finally turned to Harry. 'I'm sorry, Harry,' he said, in a heartless and unsympathetic voice. He grinned. 'At least it's close to the end of the season so you have much time to rebuild it, eh?'

He walked towards the police car and turned back. 'Listen, Harry, I'll get some of my men on it – see if we can find who did it – and why.' He closed the car door and left.

Harry spat venom. 'The bastard!' He slammed his bandaged hands on the table and immediately grimaced with pain. 'Did you see his face? He loved that. I wouldn't put it past him to have been involved.'

Nyla tried to console him. 'Mama's safe, Dad.'

Harry mumbled. 'Hmm.' He pointed his head in the direction of the tea and Nyla immediately obliged. He sipped it and took a while to regain his breath. 'Do you realise what's happened to me and my dream?' He wiped at his sore lips with his bandaged hand.

She placed her arm around his shoulder. 'I know, Baba, but it will be all right. Don't worry. You've done it once and you can do it again.'

They both looked and realised that Nyla had never referred to him in that way before. They both smiled for a split second.

Harry licked at the throbbing blisters on his lips and shook his head. 'That fire was deliberate. There was no way that could have happened on its own – by itself.' He motioned for more tea.

Nyla picked up the cup and put it to her father's lips. Harry took a sip, and tried to catch his breath before he continued. 'But who would want to do it? And why?'

Ben shook his head and spoke for the first time. 'I'm so sorry, Harry. I can help you rebuild it.'

Harry shook his head. 'I don't think so. With the EU rules that they've piled onto us, on the island, it will cost a fortune just to clear up the asbestos and get rid of it.' He wiped his eyes. 'Even if we did rebuild it we'd need to replace the kitchen equipment and fittings plus new tables and chairs.' He tried to calculate a figure in his head. 'Probably a hundred thousand euros, and that's just for starters.'

Ben looked shocked.

'And we would need somewhere to stay while we rebuild it.' Harry looked towards the still smouldering building. 'Maybe we could get a winter let.' He sat back and reflected. 'No, it's too much work.' He shook his head. 'I can't go through all that again.'

His voice faded.

Nyla cleared the table and returned with another pot of tea, two coffees and a plate of kariokes – walnut filled chocolate crescents.

While Nyla poured the tea Ben was building up the courage to speak. 'Harry.' He coughed nervously, 'I think it's time for me to go back home.'

'What about your dream to travel?' asked Nyla.

'I've had enough for a while and a fantastic experience –'

'Experience?' asked Harry.

Ben blushed. 'Well, a shock really,' he said, 'and to be honest I've grown up.' He looked at Nyla then lowered his head and sucked at the side of his mouth. 'I'm so sorry, Harry. I wish I could stay and help you.'

Harry patted his arm. 'I do too.'

Nyla took a breath before speaking out. 'Mum said I can go and stay with her if I want to.'

'Do you?'

'Yes, I think I do – for a while anyway.'

Harry lowered his head and wiped at his tearful eyes. He struggled to continue. 'Alright.' He nodded. 'Yeah, it's a good idea.' He sniffed. 'Has she agreed?'

'Yeah,' said Nyla, half-heartedly.

None of them drank their tea and coffee or touched the cakes. Ben paid and they left.

*   *   *

Harry packed his meagre smoke-damaged belongings, retrieved by the firemen, and stayed with Julian and Patricia for several weeks while he waited for news from Zavos.

Zavos finally called him and arranged to meet at a bar in the old town, and for the first time he bought Harry a coffee. 'How are you, Harry?' he asked.

Harry caught his angry reflection in Zavos's mirrored sunglasses. 'How do you think I am?'

'Erm. Well …' He hesitated and exhaled. 'I don't have any news, Harry.' He sipped at his coffee. 'We've investigated the fire. I've had four of my best men on it.'

Harry forced a tired grin. 'Zavos, I wouldn't have expected anything else.'

Zavos continued. 'But we've drawn a blank.'

Harry opened a packet of cigarettes and offered one to Zavos. He declined. Harry lit his and continued. 'Do you realise, I'm ruined?'

'Life is hard sometimes, my friend,' said Zavos.

Harry grunted.

'So, what will you do now?' asked Zavos.

'Good question,' said Harry. He finished his coffee. 'There's nothing left for me here.' He paused. 'Well, there is … Nyla … but she'll soon meet someone and get married. Who knows after that?'

Zavos stroked his moustache, alternating from side to side. Having finished preening himself he finally tilted his head and waited expectantly.

Harry continued. 'It's Christmas in a week, so maybe I'll go back to the UK and see what turns up. Life has a way of dealing us the cards and we have to make the best of them.'

He exhaled. 'I really thought I'd been dealt the best cards this time around. I love it here. But now ...' He sighed. 'It's all gone.'

Zavos fiddled with his gun holster and flicked the clip repeatedly. 'You know you made a lot of enemies here, Harry.'

Harry sniggered. 'So have you, Zavos.'

Zavos was openly ruffled and his whole body stiffened. 'I also have many friends here –'

'Friends?' snarled Harry. He slapped his thighs. 'Course you have – the people you *never* caught.'

'What are you saying, Harry?'

'Draw your own conclusions, Zavos.' Harry picked at a piece of loose skin on his top lip. 'I have mine.' He shook his head. 'You Greeks look after your own all right?'

Zavos slammed his fist on the table. 'Fuck you, Harry. *Greek?!* I'm a Greek Cypriot. What is it with you people, you think you can come to our island and do just what the hell you like?'

Harry conceded with a nod. 'Yeah, some of us do. I appreciate that, Zavos.'

Zavos stood. 'If you do decide to leave, Harry, let me have your address before you go. You never know.' He sniggered. 'Despite your cynical sentiments ...' He paused and grinned. 'We may catch whoever did it.'

He reached out his hand.

Harry reluctantly shook it but remained in his seat. 'See you, Zavos.'

Harry arranged to meet Xanthi for dinner at the Agora Tavern, situated in Kennedy Square above a sushi restaurant in the heart of old Paphos town. As well as the myriad of different sized rooms, it also had two balconies which were very popular in the summer season, a quiet terrace and roof garden. All the rooms were decorated for Christmas, with the doorways, paintings and mirrors edged with holly and branches cut from the huge Christmas tree that filled one corner of the largest room. These were hung with baubles and draped with rows of tiny bright coloured lights which dimmed and then glowed intermittently.

Harry and Xanthi chose to sit at a table in the most secluded part of the restaurant but they were unable to escape the noisy celebrations going on all around them. Harry ordered a carafe of red wine and they each ordered a salad with a twist of chickpeas, tahini which had a slight curry flavour, village halloumi and Greek souvlaki, which was slightly different to the Cypriot dish.

Harry's mood was subdued throughout the meal and he hardly touched his food or wine. While he waited for his coffee he stroked the tablecloth and fiddled with his dessert spoon.

Xanthi observed him for several minutes and heaved a sigh before speaking. 'Harry, why did you really come back?'

'We got married here. It's special,' he lied.

'Is that reason enough?' She sipped at her wine and, still holding the glass in her hand, continued. 'Why *did* we get married, Harry? You *know* you were already married –'

'What?'

'Come on, you know you were,' she said, with a laugh.

While Harry shook his head, she emptied her glass. Harry refilled it and she continued. 'So tell me, why *did* we get married?'

He lowered his head and deliberated over her question.

She continued. 'You were already married to the army – right?' She fiddled with her fork, placed it neatly to one side of her plate, and continued. 'So why did you leave me and Nyla?' She glared at him. 'How could you?'

'Xanthi, it was my dream. I was young – just a kid –'

'But you had us.'

Harry trembled. 'I know ... but once they chose *me*, I thought I was special. I wanted excitement – it's all I ever dreamed of,' he said, 'and I was hooked – they had me.' He recalled the early days in the Special Forces. 'The rush of adrenaline in Afghanistan ...' He exhaled heavily as he shook his head. 'Was fantastic.'

She grinned at him. 'And they divorced you as soon as you were no longer of any use to them, didn't they?' she said, with a grimace.

He looked at her and slowly nodded in agreement. 'Hmm. Yes, they did.'

She pushed herself back from the table and licked her lips sensually. 'Is there anyone else, Harry?'

He fidgeted nervously. 'No,' he whispered.

'Are you sure?' she asked.

He blushed and mumbled his reply. 'I was injured.'

Xanthi lowered her eyes and spoke softly. 'Oh ... I see. I'm so sorry.' She looked up at him. 'Nyla overheard what you said when she was kidnapped. Do you want to talk about it?'

Harry looked at her. 'What I will say is that it took me a long time.' He inhaled. 'Several years –'

'That bad?' she said, despairingly.

He nodded and sighed heavily before he looked towards the mirror decorated with holly and brightly coloured flashing plastic fruit. 'The doctors said I'd never walk again.'

Xanthi gasped.

Harry closed his eyes once more and sucked at his bottom lip. 'That's what they said.' He smiled. 'But I proved the bastards wrong.' He shrugged. 'And here I am. Well.' He reflected as he patted his chest pocket and continued. 'Well … almost as good as new.' He pulled a small plastic bottle from the pocket and shook it.

She tried to read the label but it wasn't possible.

'Morphine,' he said, as he squeezed the bottle tightly in his hand. 'I take them most days.'

She reached out and rubbed his hand. 'I'm sorry, Harry. I didn't know.' She shook her head in disbelief. 'I never realised.'

'Hmm. Why would you?' He looked away. 'No worries. I was born to walk the wire – it taught me lessons in life.' He sniffed. 'Well, there you are.' He looked into her eyes. 'Happy now?'

She didn't reply.

He straightened his neck and lifted his chin. 'Anyway.' He lit a cigarette and exhaled a thick cloud of smoke before speaking. 'I've given it a lot of thought.' He took another extended drag and exhaled. He spoke through the smoke. 'I'm going back to England '

'Now?' asked Xanthi.

He nodded and tapped the cigarette on the edge of the large ash tray. 'Zavos hasn't got a clue who did it, or so he says.' He forced a contemptuous smile. 'What have I got left here after the fire?' He took several more huge drags. He continued coyly. 'Nothing … there's no insurance and I don't have the money to rebuild it. So what else can I do?'

Xanthi frowned at him. 'Nothing?! Are you sure, you really *mean* that?'

Harry snapped at her. 'That's right. I said ... *nothing.*' He stroked his nose and sniffed hard at the same time. He rubbed at his eyes as he tried to hold back a tear. 'You know there's nothing for me here now.'

'Have you forgotten, Nyla – *your* daughter?'

He glared at her. 'Course not. How could I ever do that?'

'Well, you seem to –'

'No. I haven't.' He shook his head wildly. 'And I can't take her to England. What would she do?' He paused and looked at her inquisitively.

She placed her elbow on the table and slid her left hand across her mouth while she tried to think of a solution.

Harry took his time to scrutinise her delicate fingers, her wedding ring, and her brightly painted, manicured nails. 'Hmm,' he said, as he mirrored her gesture before pinching the stubble on his chin. 'I have nowhere to live and no job, so ...' He sighed as he removed his hand from his mouth and, with his elbow still resting on the table, left his open palm poised in mid-air. 'No income. Does that tell you why?' He sighed heavily. 'And, something you seem to have overlooked.'

He stared directly at her and gave her time to think about what he'd said.

She didn't reply but questioned him silently with a slight flick of her head.

Harry continued. 'Has it honestly occurred to you? I'm broke. End of story. It's a no-brainer. Right?'

She fiddled with her unused dessert fork and looked over his head. 'Yeah. OK.' She pushed her plate away. 'So, will you tell her?'

Harry sighed heavily and forced his reply. 'I'd rather not.'

'Did you hear what you just said?' She cursed. 'Do you

mean that?' He nodded. 'So what the hell am I supposed to tell *your* daughter?!' She made to stand. 'You're leaving that to me.' She exhaled her anger. 'You come back into her life after twenty years and just as quickly ...' She took a huge breath and continued. 'You choose to disappear.'

'Xanthi, I didn't choose to disappear this time, did I?'

She agreed with a token shrug. 'OK, Harry.'

He stretched out his arms, turned up his palms, blew out his cheeks, and as he exhaled he mouthed his apology.

Xanthi stood and threw her serviette onto the table and screamed back at him as she stormed out of the restaurant. 'Fuck you, Harry Clark! Or, whoever you are!'

He ignored the looks from the waiters and customers sitting at the other tables and took his time to finish his cigarette.

Harry, his hand poised above the ashtray, was about to stub out his cigarette. He looked up to see Xanthi standing in front of him. He gazed up at her open-mouthed.

She opened her handbag and removed a tiny photograph from the plastic wallet. She handed it to him. 'You can have this,' she said. 'OK?'

He looked at the photo of himself with Xanthi and the day old Nyla in the maternity ward.

Xanthi said, 'Look after yourself,' she said. She kissed him on the cheek and left.

He rubbed at his eyes as he paid the bill before walking out into the night and taking a taxi to the airport and a plane to Luton airport.

CHAPTER EIGHTEEN

Since You've Been Gone

The hire car shot up the drive of the semi-detached house, crushing the remnants of the crisp autumn leaves under its wheels, before stopping. Harry walked slowly towards the front door, checked his keys, and entered. The house was cold and empty, not something he had been used to. In the silence, he stood looking around the room; the silver Christmas tree in pride of place in the corner, the cards placed symmetrically around every inch of wall and the brightly wrapped presents beneath the television. He reached forward and read several of the cards slowly to himself before wiping the tears from his eyes. In a split second he took in every detail before slipping awkwardly into a large threadbare armchair.

'Why?' he asked.

He paused and looked around before repeating his question. 'What is wrong with me?' he screamed. 'Everything I touch gets fucked up.'

Two days earlier, on Christmas Eve, Harry had returned to England and arrived at his widowed mother's London home.

He struggled with his bags. His arms were full of Christmas presents and a carefully chosen fresh turkey with all the trimmings. He had arranged to stay with his mother for a while to give him time to decide what he was going to do next. There was no reply to his soft repetitive rapping on the door and after repeating it several times he decided to use his key. He walked into the hall, wiped his feet several times and called out. 'Mum ... are you there?'

He could hear the carols coming from her DAB radio, a present that his mother really appreciated following the death of his father. He walked into the sitting room, where flames reflected from the coal fire created flickering patterns around the room. He walked in and out to the kitchen where the radio played to itself.

In a state of unbelieving panic, he ran upstairs.

Nothing.

Where was she?

He ran down the stairs and into the sitting room and turned on the light. His eyes flitted around the room. Then he saw her. His mother was slumped forward in her favourite arm-chair facing towards the fire.

'Mum ... are you alright? Come on, Mum – is this some sort of joke?'

He felt her hands – they were cold.

He let out a blood-curdling scream. 'God help me!'

Crying, he reached deep into his pocket for his mobile and dialled.

Within ten minutes the paramedics arrived and confirmed what he already knew.

'Can I have a few minutes on my own with her?' asked Harry, through the tears.

'Of course you can,' said the most senior of the two paramedics.

'No problem,' said the female, smiling her understanding to him.

The house was strangely quiet as he carefully removed the cards from the mantlepiece and then those stuck to the wall with blu tack before starting to strip the Christmas tree. As he carefully removed each decoration he cupped it in his hand and studied it. He remembered them all, even the withered pine cones he had collected from Epping Forest when he was at primary school, and had painted gold and silver before proudly presenting them to his mother and father at the end of the autumn term. He remembered each of the wafer thin glass baubles that were antiques even before he was born and the wooden decorations that his father had painstakingly carved and then painted for his third Christmas.

Every decoration had a story and he knew them all.

He removed the last decoration and, holding it carefully in his hand, he sat down and cried uncontrollably. The decoration had no more significance than any other but it was the last and he knew this was the end of something that had been part of his life for as long as he could remember. Now it had suddenly ended. Painstakingly, he packed them all into a plastic container, closed the lid, and put it in the spare bedroom.

CHAPTER NINETEEN

Starting Over

When his mother died he moved into the house and took a job as a security guard for a private company, where he worked transporting prisoners to court hearings across London and occasionally to other parts of England.

Harry drove a prisoner from London to attend an identity parade in Devon but the early Easter bank holiday traffic extended what was a five hour journey to seven. By the time he reached Tavistock the witnesses had returned to Plymouth. The station duty officer booked him into the eighteenth century Bedford Hotel across the road from the station. He had an early dinner and decided to explore the moor. He left Tavistock, drove up onto the moor and through Princetown. After driving for several more miles he parked up in a lane to enjoy the last of the evening sun. He lit a cigarette and walked down the lane until he reached a broken five bar gate. On the granite post was a faded wooden name board, *"Redwing Cottage."* He pushed open the broken gate and walked down the grass covered track. What he saw that evening was his new dream, a derelict cottage with an overgrown garden. On one side was a large copse which fell within the barbed wire boundary, and there was a narrow stream which was one of many tributaries of the River Dart.

The next morning he was up early and visited West Devon Council offices. They put him in touch with the farmer that owned the cottage and adjoining woods. By the time the prisoner had been positively identified and was ready to be driven back to London, Harry had agreed on a price with the farmer. Five weeks later Redwing Cottage was his. He sold his parents' house in London and used some of the money to pay for the cottage and materials to renovate what would be his new home.

Harry had always dreamed of living in the country but, for a few long minutes, the overnight snow had caused him to perhaps question his decision.

Walking into the newly decorated sitting room he stood for a moment and smiled to himself, proud that at last he had completed the almost impossible task of single-handedly renovating the shell of a cottage. He had had to clean layers of thick mud from the floors, chip away the cement and concrete covering the flagstone floor before finally taking it up and cleaning every piece by hand, then relaying the random hand cut pieces. The oak beams had been stripped of coat upon coat of black paint and then waxed. The walls stripped back to the original lathes, replastered, then along with the ceiling redecorated in complementary pastel shades. Despite his original idea to go back to basics and not to install any modern amenities, except hot running water and electricity, he soon abandoned his plans and installed the obligatory electrical appliances, fridge, freezer and microwave, and in pride of place a Rayburn oven. But with the advent of the cold autumn winds and icy rain he was forced to change his mind again after dreading to walk anywhere on the cold ground floor barefoot. He gave in, drove across the moor to Moretonhampstead, and bought a large handmade Bakhtiar Persian rug which now obliterated the majority of his efforts. The finishing touch completed what was without doubt a warm and cosy hideaway as soon as he locked the doors and lit the open fire in his lounge.

By the time Harry woke up and looked out of his bedroom window, the snow was nearly eighteen inches deep and his reconditioned 1988, "E" reg, Land Rover was consumed up to the axles in white virgin snow.

He quickly dressed, rushed down to the kitchen, filled and boiled the kettle and poured the steaming liquid onto the coffee granules.

After rubbing the condensation off the timber kitchen window, carefully avoiding the unusual and colourful exotic plants on the cill, Harry stared silently out at what had been an unexpected transformation. He sipped occasionally at the hot liquid while he contemplated his next move.

He looked around the room, checking his watch with the reproduction grandfather clock in the corner, the only modern piece in a room furnished with the antique furniture he had bought, even before he had completed his renovation work, at an auction in Tavistock Town Hall.

He strode towards the wide granite fireplace and, reaching down, grabbed the carved wooden handle of the poker. He pushed haphazardly at the ashes before carefully selecting several suitable logs from the large wicker basket. He took care to place the largest and heaviest log onto the remaining glowing embers. He stood at the door and returned to place the fireguard across the open fireplace before taking one final look at the fire before walking back into the hall. He sat on the open wooden staircase and pulled on his leather boots before he stood up and grabbed at the heavy ankle length overcoat hanging behind the door. He pulled it over his broad shoulders. While he wound the well-worn scarf around his neck, he took a deep breath and talked to himself. 'Let's get on with it,' he said, unconvincingly.

He stood up and pulled on his black hand-stitched leather gloves, one of the few possessions he'd brought back from Cyprus, before unbolting the front door and walking out into what was a winter wonderland.

By the time he reached his Land Rover the snow had stopped and the weak early morning sun was already break-ing through the snow covered branches of the tall pine trees on one side of his cottage. He took in the stillness, looked back towards the cottage and smiled at the smoke as it floated out of the tall, granite chimney, and high into the clear blue windless sky.

Harry experienced a mixed sense of achievement and euphoria as he finally realised that he should never have doubted his motives for moving. But a split second later he crouched cautiously beside the vehicle, his razor sharp senses reacting to the unusual sound. Once he had established the cause of the distraction, a lone distressed blackbird as it landed heavily on a nearby branch creating a cloud of powdery snow, his body began to relax and he turned his attention to the rusty disfigured vehicle. He brushed the soft powdery snow from the windscreen and the other windows, and within a few minutes he was sitting inside. He flicked the ignition key. The engine turned over and started immediately, breaking the silence of the new dawn. The heater fan cut in, whirring and rattling loudly. 'I must get that fixed,' he promised himself.

Beginning to feel the cold, he moaned, turned on the radio and sat as the pathetic heater tried unsuccessfully to warm the freezing air and clear the ice from the inside of the windscreen.

He effortlessly pushed in the worn clutch and edged the vehicle down the narrow track towards the "B" road that cut its way through the forest and into town. Even this well-used road was almost untouched as he drove slowly, violating the virgin snow with the wide, thick treaded tyres of his vehicle.

By the time he reached Tavistock the majority of roads in the centre had been cleared and the council workers were busy shovelling the snow from the pavements around the market square.

Tavistock police station and the buildings around it were very unusual, constructed of locally quarried granite and built to resemble a moorland castle; it blended in almost unnoticed amongst the other identically constructed buildings that formed the centre of this idyllic moorland town. The police station had already been reduced to admin offices only, relying on emergency phone calls to Plymouth or Exeter, and was due for imminent closure. The buildings were unique and two gateways, Court Gate and Betsy Grimbal's Tower, from the unique sixteenth century buildings remained. A ruined arch from the Still Tower, where the monks made their medicines, beside the River Tavy, still stood. When Henry VIII dissolved the monasteries, he gave Tavistock Abbey and all of the surrounding land to the Russell family, who later became the

Dukes of Bedford. In 1860, Francis, the fifth Duke of Bedford, made a fortune from copper mining and rebuilt the centre of Tavistock and built cottages for the miners.

He drove along the river, turned into the public car park at the front of the police station, and through the carved granite arch before parking outside of the rear entrance.

The town was usually quiet this time of the morning but today it was even more so. Harry liked it that way.

CHAPTER TWENTY

More Than A Feeling

Harry kept in contact with Nyla via Skype on his laptop and they talked every Friday.

His laptop pinged.

This was Wednesday.

He sat down in his favourite armchair and placed his coffee on the table beside him.

Nyla appeared on his screen.

'Hi, Dad, how are you?'

'It's Wednesday.'

'I know.'

'It's good to hear from you but why call me tonight?'

'I saw him.'

Harry could see that she was frightened.

'Saw who?'

'That man –'

'What man?'

'The man who was stabbed in the warehouse –'

'Are you sure?'

'Yes, I am.'

'Where?'

'I was having lunch with Mum at one of the restaurants on the quayside today and he came by in his Mercedes.'

Harry fired Nyla a series of questions. 'Was he driving? Was it him? Are you sure?'

Nyla suddenly appeared to have some doubt.

'Well I thought I saw him a few weeks ago but wasn't sure. But today I recognised his driver and his car.'

'Are you sure?'

She hesitated. 'Yeah ...' She paused. 'I could never forget that bastard –'

He raised his voice to her. 'Don't swear. Understand. There is no need for that.'

'Sorry, Dad.'

Silence.

Nyla gushed. 'I got his car number –'

'What?'

Harry drummed his fingers impatiently on the arm of the settee. 'How?' he asked.

'When I saw him today I had a good look at his driver, then I knew it was him for sure. When they parked the car I sneaked over and got the registration number.'

Renewed silence.

Harry didn't hide his impatience. 'Come on then –'

'Come on what, Dad?'

'Give it to me.'

She read out the car registration and Harry wrote it down while he talked to her.

'Are you still staying with your mother?'

'Yeah.'

'Well, make sure you stay with her.'

'Dad, you're worrying me.'

'There's no need to be worried.' He paused. 'Take care and make sure you stay with your mother. Right?'

'OK. But I wish you were here.'

'You'll be fine.' He paused and lowered his voice 'Love you, Nyla,' he said, for only the second time in her life.

He cut the call, made another coffee, and spent the next hour trawling the web and scribbling in his notebook.

Harry went to his shed and took out two six-inch wallpaper scrapers and a roll of stained linen. He walked back to the lounge and, unusually for him, pulled the curtains, then dimmed the lights. He stood in front of his granite fireplace and tapped his fingers on the shelf. He had deliberately not pointed it and had laid out the left-hand side of the stonework around the open fireplace to reflect, to him, a clock face. He placed the linen around the end of the paint scrapers and, taking care not to make any marks, he pushed them between the two joints at 12:45 on the invisible clock. He then carefully removed the scrapers and gently pulled the linen, which had hooked itself to the rough edges of the granite. The stone moved and he was able to grip the edges and slide it out, revealing a small safe. He flicked the combination and opened the door. He removed the first passport and flicked it open. He stared at the picture and felt the twinge of excitement run through his body as he talked to himself. 'Hello, Stryker. Good to have you back,' he said, with a smile in his voice. He wanted to use Stryker's passport but knew he could be traced if he did.

He exhaled before reluctantly putting it back in the safe and taking out two passports which had been forged for him eighteen months earlier in Cyprus. He knew that he had to remain anonymous during his visit and they would help him to achieve that. He would use one passport to travel to Cyprus and the other one on the return flight.

He grabbed a handful of used euro notes, a few coins and the driving licences in the same names as the passports. He packed a few things in a canvas shoulder bag and drove to his office where he made a search on the police computer before driving to Exeter and taking a bus to Bristol airport. He used his first false passport and, paying in cash, bought a one-way ticket with easyJet to fly the four and a half hours to Paphos National Airport.

CHAPTER TWENTY-ONE

Travelling Light

Harry arrived in Cyprus as it was getting dark. He passed through immigration without any problems and stood in the airport car park. He shivered as he realised how cold it could be that time of year. Years earlier, he had spent every hour renovating the building that was to become his home and bar and he didn't notice it then. So many people on the island knew him but this time he wanted to remain as invisible as possible. He was on a mission and surprise was the key.

He took the shuttle minibus into Kato, approximately twenty minutes from the centre of Paphos, and made for the large commercial unit that hired motorcycles and mountain bikes to tourists as well as selling outdoor sports equipment. It was now deserted and closed for the winter. He walked around the perimeter of the building, disabled the security cameras, and broke in. Once inside, he deactivated what was a very basic alarm system and made his choice of motorcycle – a Honda Shadow, 750cc, Africa Twin, and filled the fuel tank. He picked his way between the rows of brightly coloured clothes and motorcycle gear and chose a set of plain black leathers and a black crash helmet with a black tinted, full face visor. He grabbed a black rucksack and took his time walking along the aisles filling it with everything he wanted. He removed the few items he needed from his canvas travel bag, sliding them in the side pockets of the rucksack, and hid it beneath a pile of innocuous cardboard boxes, ripped and blood stained Kevlars.

Using his office computer in Tavistock police station he had been able to trace Malik, as the registered owner of the car, to his address in Cyprus. He checked it on the map and travelled out of Paphos and through Polemi, a village with a population of less than a thousand people, set on a plateau overlooking farmland in the valleys either side of it. He continued up into the hills until he reached Psathi, an even smaller village which overlooked the beautiful Happy Valley.

He was already waiting for Malik when Raheem indicated and turned the shiny black Mercedes into the curved drive. The car drove to the end of the row of four identical bungalows and reversed into the drive. The security lights immediately lit up the whole area around the property.

Harry was stunned at what he saw.

Raheem opened the boot and took out a wheelchair. He pushed it to the rear passenger door and strained as he man-handled Malik into it. The Iraqi's weight had ballooned to more than eighteen stone and he was totally incapable of walking. His full-faced, bushy grey beard made him almost unrecognisable to most people, but Harry could never forget his long-time adversary.

Harry fought hard to hold back a satiating grin while he watched Raheem push Malik into the rear garden and through sliding patio doors, which overlooked the swimming pool, and into the bungalow.

After checking his watch, Harry re-entered the garage of the empty holiday bungalow, conveniently situated next door to Malik, where he had already placed his rucksack in the roof space and hidden his motorbike. He waited until the security lights went out and pushed his motorbike onto the main road before firing it up and riding off.

He returned by taxi, close to midnight, and slept until he heard movement next door. Guided by the time Nyla had seen Malik in Paphos, he knew that it would be nearer to lunch-time before they left for his favourite taverna which overlooked Paphos harbour.

He watched Raheem push Malik out of the bungalow, help him out of the wheelchair, and hoist him into the car. An exhausted Malik slumped into the rear seat and immediately closed his eyes. Raheem walked the wheelchair towards the boot. He flicked it open and after closing the wheelchair he lifted it into the boot. While Raheem was preoccupied, Harry struck him in the centre of his right temple with his clenched nitrile black, latex gloved, fist. He crumbled to the gravel, unconscious. He removed Raheem's jacket, put it on, and checked the pockets for his gun. He picked up his chauffeur's cap from the gravel car park and, after beating off the dust, he put it on. He forced Raheem's flaccid body on top of the wheelchair and closed the boot. He adjusted the chauffeur's jacket and realigned the cap before walking around the car and sliding into the driver's seat.

Harry drove down the B7 for almost thirty miles until he was close to the coast. He slowed down, turned to face Malik, and slowly removed the chauffeur's cap.

Malik had immediately noticed the black latex gloves but waited until the driver spoke to him before feigning surprise. 'Hello, Harry,' he drawled. 'Fancy seeing you again.'

Harry managed an initial grunt. 'Well, Malik I see you are a survivor too.' Harry adjusted the rear view mirror and took a closer look at Malik. 'You've put on weight.'

Malik grinned back into the rear mirror. 'Maybe a little ...,' he cackled. He paused to catch his breath before he finished his sentence. 'Harry.'

Harry sniggered as he tried to come to terms with his huge adversary in the back seat.

Malik made use of Harry's apparently relaxed demeanour and whilst he took his time to regain his breath he sent a short text on his mobile before turning it off and thrusting it deep down the side of the leather seat. He continued with slurred words 'Thanks to that kid, I was laid up – have been for months.'

Harry shot him a satisfied smile. 'I thought you were dead, Malik,' he said, emphasising the word "dead."

Malik coughed a deep chesty cough. 'Yeah. So did everyone else.' He grinned. 'But I made it too, Harry.'

Harry grunted briefly until a huge smile crossed his face. 'To fight another day?'

Malik continued. 'Not now I'm in that fucking chariot.'

Harry stifled a grin. 'I got out of mine.'

'I won't,' said Malik. He coughed. 'I won't be getting out of it.'

Harry's face exploded with a gash of a smile. 'Wh ... ?'

Malik took a shallow breath before he continued. 'I had a fucking stroke.'

Harry smirked. 'Now you know what I went through.'

Malik grunted. 'You're a tough one, Harry?'

Harry gritted his teeth. 'It's not about being tough, it's about determination and strength,' he said, as he remembered his battle against the odds to walk and make a recovery from his appalling injuries. He gazed out of the window at the dark threatening sky on the horizon. 'Looks like rain.'

Malik grunted his indifference.

Harry braked to a halt and stared at him. 'Did you order it?'

'Order what?'

'Firebombing my bar –'

'No. It wasn't me,' said Malik, shaking his head vehemently. He let out a mischievous chuckle. 'But I must say – I did think about it.'

Harry depressed the clutch and gunned the accelerator.

'But why would I order that, Harry?' He paused. 'I mean …' He exhaled. 'It's not very inventive is it?'

Harry released the clutch and Malik was thrown violently back in his seat.

'Who did it?'

'Check out the bastards at the Harbour Side taverna.'

'Really?' Harry slowed down and took his time to study Malik in the rear view mirror. 'You're not giving me any more of your shit, are you, Malik?'

'Why would I do that, Harry?' He laughed loudly. 'After all …' He paused. 'We are honourable men, are we not?'

Harry turned and shot him a derisive look before he continued to drive towards the coast, and the last of the late afternoon sun as it edged through the ever diminishing breaks in the heavy rain bearing clouds.

'I'm not in any position to do otherwise? Am I?' slurred

Malik. He coughed while he laughed. 'Maybe order yourself a pizza while you're there.'

'Where?'

He huffed. 'The Harbour Side – I just told you.'

Harry shook his head and drove along the coast towards the headland that overlooked Chlorakas Beach. As he took in the beautiful deserted coastline he flicked through the CD collection in the tray beside him. He turned to Malik. 'Is there anything in here you like?'

'Music?' Malik's sombre face took on an absurd smile. 'What the fuck, Harry?' He raised his top lip in disgust as he spewed his anger. 'Music? Have you gone soft?' He shook his head to reinforce his revulsion. 'Raheem was the music lover. Not me,' he snarled.

Harry ignored his passenger and pulled a CD from his pocket and slid it into the player. He waited for it to load and flicked through the menu until he found a specific track. The distinctive electro drum loop, ethereal guitar, and haunting keyboards, followed by the fragile and tortured, echoed voice of Phil Collins, filled the car.

While *In The Air Tonight* played, Harry took time to reflect on the fitting lyrics.

Malik was the first to speak. 'Come on. Are you going to drop me, Harry?' he coughed. 'What about – honour – respect?'

'You have no idea what honour is,' screamed Harry.

Malik grinned back at him and clicked his tongue.

'Do you, Malik?'

Malik shrugged.

Harry continued. 'For all those years ...' He paused and reflected. 'When I eventually got to close my eyes at night – all I saw was your fucking face.'

Malik cocked his head and shot him a look of arrogant satisfaction.

Harry continued. 'And, it drove me crazy.'

As the drums kicked in, Harry nudged the player up to full volume.

Malik closed his eyes, covered his ears, and pressed himself deep into his seat as he tried to escape the torturous musical onslaught.

When the track finished Harry flicked off the player.

In the contrasting silence, the car turned along the cliff path until it reached the headland that jutted out into one of the deepest parts of the Mediterranean around the island. Harry had chosen the deserted location specifically for the deep water. He killed the engine, got out of the car, placed Raheem's mobile on the top of an easily identified rock, slid into the rear seat of the car and squeezed next to Malik.

Malik knew Harry was going to kill him but he didn't think he would do it with his bare hands. Nevertheless, beads of sweat appeared across his tortured forehead.

'OK, Malik.' Harry sighed. 'I'm tired too.' He took a deep breath and spoke as he exhaled. 'Just tell me, who was the shadow?'

Malik shook his head and shot him a puzzled look.

Harry shuffled uncomfortably in the leather seat.

Malik smirked at him. 'Come on, Harry.' Malik tutted. 'You know who it was.'

Harry tilted his head back, rested it on the headrest, and closed his eyes. He took a deep breath before he spoke. 'The bastard.' He exhaled. 'Who was it that took me down in that bunker?'

Malik ignored him and pulled the gold case from his inside

jacket pocket but, after taking his time to remove a cigarette, he struggled to light it.

Harry grabbed the lighter from Malik and lit it for him.

'You still want to be in control, eh, Harry?'

Harry helped himself to a cigarette, snapped the case closed and rammed it awkwardly into Malik's jacket pocket. He let his tongue glide along his dry bottom lip before sliding the cigarette into his mouth and taking his time to light it. He took a huge drag and blew the smoke directly into Malik's face.

Malik coughed and fought to catch his breath.

Harry grinned.

Malik looked down at Harry's latex gloved hands. 'Why the gloves, uh, Harry?'

Harry took another heavy drag and followed the smoke as it left his mouth. He removed the cigarette from his mouth and licked both lips. 'No one ...' He looked hard at Malik. 'I mean no one ... will ever know I came back.' He grinned and rubbed his gloves together. 'Well, not this time anyway.'

Malik grinned. 'You've got it all worked out, eh?'

Harry took his time to nod his reply. 'Uh-huh.'

Malik wheezed as he spoke. 'I'm dying, Harry.'

'I know you are, Malik,' he said condescendingly.

'We're all going to die one day, Harry,' said Malik. He took a drag. 'Some sooner than others I suppose.'

Harry mumbled and took several drags while he looked out of the window. 'So – I'll ask you again. Who ... was the fucking shadow?'

Malik, now short of breath, grunted his reply and managed another drag of his diminishing cigarette.

Harry could hear the congestion gurgling in his lungs.

'Look at you. Do you realise, I could be doing you a favour, Malik.'

Malik shrugged indifferently. 'Um.'

'So ... who was it?'

'*I* will never tell you that,' replied Malik, with utter contempt in his voice.

Harry jumped out of the car, slammed the door, stamped out his cigarette on the rocks, and returned to the driver's seat. He turned the ignition key and started the car. He hit out at the CD player before flicking at four switches. The electric windows slid down and, on cue Phil Collins began to sing.

Harry reversed as far as he could and waited until the legendary drum passage thundered out of the speakers. He revved the engine as much as he dared and raced the car along the uneven rocky outcrop. When he reached the cliff edge he pushed the accelerator pedal down to the floor. The car flew silently into the air before belly-flopping into the Mediterranean. He waited patiently for the car to fill with the cold sea water and when it reached his shoulders he turned to Malik. 'You didn't need to tell me.' His face took on a confident grin. 'I know who the bloody shadow is.'

Malik frowned and was quiet for a long moment.

Harry continued. 'I just wanted to see if you were, as you put it, an "honourable man."'

Malik shot him an inane grin, raised his open hands and turned them, palm up.

Harry flicked a couple of switches and the doors clicked.

Locked.

Malik knew there was no way he could escape even if he was able to swim.

Harry fumbled under the dashboard and unlocked the boot,

which immediately flooded, and the car began to level out. As the water reached Harry's neck he took a huge gulp of air and pushed himself out through the driver's window. He swam around to the open boot and pulled out Raheem, dragged him through the water and forced him feet first through the driver's window.

Harry held his breath while he maintained his steely stare on Malik. He watched as the water licked around the Iraqi's neck. Even now, he still appeared to remain composed. He pushed the cigarette between his teeth, crossed his arms, and sat calmly in his seat.

Malik smiled to himself and smirked defiantly at Harry.

Harry gave his longtime adversary a final glance and mouthed to him. 'Fuck you.'

As the water licked around Malik's nose, he pushed his head into the headrest, and took one last drag on his cigarette through his teeth. The rising water extinguished it with an insignificant hiss. Malik released the spent cigarette butt and watched it float above his head before it drifted through the nearest open window. He tilted his head as far back as he could, took one final gasp of air through his nose, and held it in his damaged lungs until the water enveloped his head.

Malik exhaled for the last time.

Harry powered to the surface and gulped at the air before swimming to the deserted shore. He walked along the rocks and picked up Raheem's mobile phone. He stood on the beach and waited until the last of the air bubbles reached the surface. When he was satisfied the car was on the sea bed, he took his time to walk up the pebble beach to the dilapidated fisherman's hut and the motorbike he had hidden the previous evening. As he took in the last of the sporadic evening sun, he kicked blindly at the pebbles and thought about what he had just achieved. He was not experiencing the euphoria he had expected. He already knew he was long past that.

He pulled on his black leather trousers, jacket, boots, helmet and a new pair of latex gloves.

He felt good.

He was now on a new mission and what would be an unforeseen fulfilment of his retribution.

Harry adjusted his motorcycle helmet, flicked down the visor and fired up the stolen motorcycle. He revved it up until he could feel the power throbbing between his thighs. He rode into Paphos, along the harbourside towards the breakwater and his decimated bar. He parked his motorbike at the ripped and faded police cordon tape. He slipped beneath it and took his time to walk closer to the charred building.

He shuddered as he remembered how his dream had died with the fire.

He flicked up the dark visor and brushed the tears from his eyes.

The few undamaged seats and tables were positioned where they were left after the fire, more than a year earlier. The overhead bamboo screening had been totally destroyed and now lay draped unevenly across many of the twisted seats and tables. The grapevines that he had so lovingly tended throughout the hot summer had all but died. The few vines that remained were dry and the grapes had withered except for a couple of hardy bare branches. The fibreglass hot tub, filled with smashed roof tiles and lengths of twisted and burnt timber, had melted from the intense heat and was distorted into a twisted and unrecognisable shape. The dirty water trickled through the holes and drained out over Harry's boots as he passed.

The main roof of the building had collapsed and, as Harry kicked at the front door, pigeons roosting inside scattered noisily above him. He desperately wanted to go inside but thought better of it, instead he brushed off a chair etched with the corrosive ash and sat down. While he smoked a cigarette he changed his mind and made his way through the debris. He fought with himself as he entered the building for the first time since the fire. He inhaled sharply and fought off the intense feeling of despair. He found it hard to take in the devastation. Everything was coated in thick black soot and ash. The distorted and rusting metal frame of the piano looked strangely bizarre on the collapsed stage. The optics behind the bar had melted and twisted into weird shapes and now hung precariously from the misshapen metal brackets. The remainder of the ceiling that he had so sympathetically crafted was no more than charred deformed framework. When he picked up a black smoke-stained glass from the bar it left a perfect circle of shiny varnished timber. He trembled as he ran his finger around the circle and along the thick ash on the bar. The blackened mirror behind the bar was streaked with ripples of black and silver, where the water from the fire hoses and rain had run down the glass. Some of the sullied pictures had fallen from the wall leaving surreal but perfect and clean stuccoed rectangles behind them. Most of the seats and tables were twisted and the remaining armchairs and settees were now little more than blackened metal frames. He finally walked into the remnants of his workshop. He trembled and wiped at his tears as he slowly took in the horrendous devastation around him. He removed a stone in the wall and turned the tumbler. A small steel fireproof door opened. Harry removed some of his very special objects and closed it. He slipped them into the pockets of his rucksack and walked towards the door.

His shattered dream still affected him.

He took his time to reflect on when his bar was a hive of activity, but the rolling thunder out at sea dragged him back. His state of mind was unimaginable but reality kicked in when he looked out at the darkening sky and the heavy clouds that rushed towards him.

He pulled up his collar.

All he wanted now was revenge.

CHAPTER TWENTY-TWO

Everybody Hurts

Savina's mobile pinged and she read the message on the screen. She raced into the kitchen where Yanis stood over the gas cooker preparing an all-day full English breakfast for an elderly ex-pat. She passed him the phone and quaked uncontrollably as she waited for him to read the message.

> **Good evening**
> **I hope you're well.**
> **I'm coming to see you.**

Yanis bit at his bottom lip and his face drained of all colour. He looked back at Savina and repeated the message over and over in his mind. He threw down the spatula and turned off the gas. 'We go now,' he said, as he yanked at the cords of his apron, dragged it over his head, and threw it onto the floor.

'Now?'

'Yes. We go now – this minute,' he said. He couldn't hide the panic in his voice. 'Go and pack a few things.' He physically shook with fear. 'Get our passports and ... and ... and take all the money from the safe.'

Savina raced up the stairs.

He shouted after her. 'Call a taxi.'

'Where?' she asked.

He roared after her. 'The *airport* – where else?'

She dialled her mobile and tossed a few useless items into a small travel bag while she waited for an answer. She threw open the safe door, grabbed their passports and all the cash they possessed, then ordered a taxi. She crammed the cash and passports into her handbag and blindly grabbed two jackets, a t-shirt and a pair of jeans from the wardrobe.

Yanis was waiting at the bottom of the stairs and had already cajoled their disgruntled customers into leaving.

Savina looked at his chef's clothes.

'Let's go.' He shook his head. 'Come on. I'll change in the taxi.'

Savina handed Yanis his jacket, jeans, t-shirt and passport, then checked her purse to make sure she had their credit cards. Yanis reached out and grabbed the cash. She watched him count the large denomination euro notes before jamming them back into her handbag.

After hurriedly locking the front taverna doors they climbed into the waiting taxi.

'Airport,' barked Yanis.

The leather-clad motorcyclist appeared from nowhere and thrust his crash helmeted head through the taxi drivers open window. He motioned to him to turn off his radio.

The driver shook his head in defiance and turned it up.

The helmet smashed into his nose.

The driver leaned forward and turned off the radio. He

winced at the pain, and moaned while he wiped at his blood covered face.

Silence.

The motorcyclist spoke directly to the taxi driver in Greek. 'You're cancelled.' He peered through his visor at the passengers sitting in the rear seat. 'Out – NOW!'

The driver grunted at them.

Yanis and Savina opened the rear doors and unable to hide their dread, they slowly climbed out.

The motorcyclist handed the taxi driver a fifty euro note and, after pushing it into his shirt pocket, he raced away.

Yanis and Savina stood nervously on the pavement. And a cold hard rain began to fall onto the now deserted streets.

'Inside,' roared the stranger.

Yanis appeared to offer resistance by clenching his fists but before he could muster the courage to strike out the man smacked him across the head with his open gloved hand.

'I said ... inside.' The man pulled out Raheem's revolver, a 9mm Glock 17, and primed it before pointing it menacingly at each of them.

Thunder crashed and the torrential rain hammered down onto the chairs and tables that now looked strangely out of place outside of their abandoned taverna. The rain cascaded from their plastic canopy and ran like a river across the pavement. The motorcyclist looked up at the CCTV cameras that had been turned off since the last of the tourists departed at the start of winter, when the majority of the bars had chosen to close at the same time. Still holding the gun he used it to direct Savina and Yanis towards the locked door.

Yanis shook and fumbled with the key as he tried to slip it into the lock.

The man grabbed at Savina's left arm and twisted it violently. She let out a pained scream.

The leather-clad man released her arm and covered her mouth with his free hand.

She tried desperately to breathe through the latex glove.

After a few desperate seconds Yanis finally unlocked the aluminium doors and slid them open.

The man motioned to him to relock the doors and gestured to him to pull down the roller blinds. He forced them through the restaurant, past the tables with plates of half-eaten food and part finished tea and coffee, and up the stairs to the first floor flat.

He turned on the lights and grabbed two chairs from the dining table and placed them back to back. Without saying a word he motioned to them to sit down.

They refused.

He smacked each of them across the head with the back of his gloved hand and they obliged by reluctantly sitting down. He turned his back on them, removed his rucksack, and took his time to remove his crash helmet, which he set on the table beside his rucksack. He flicked through the numerous pockets and lined up some of the contents on the table before he turned to face them.

When they saw his face they began to relax.

Yanis managed a smile. 'Hello, Harry,' he said.

'How are you,' asked Savina patronisingly.

Harry grunted his reply.

He grabbed the nylon rope, fashioned a noose and placed it around both of their necks. He pulled it tight and wrapped the end around his left hand. 'Take off your clothes,' he said, in a restrained and measured voice.

They looked at him and simultaneously shook their heads.

He suddenly lost his patience and, unable to control his pent-up anger any longer, struck out at them. 'You heard what I said. Do it. NOW!'

'Come on, Harry. Why are you doing this?' asked Savina, taking her time to force a smile.

He snarled at her before turning his attention to Yanis. 'Just do it.'

Yanis took his time to kick off his trainers before reaching for his leather belt. He undid it and dropped his black and white check chef's trousers. He removed his food stained t-shirt and threw it defiantly across the room.

Harry tugged hard on the rope and they both fell to the floor. 'Get up.' They took their time to get to their feet. He pointed at Savina. 'Now you.'

She looked at him and quivered. 'Me?'

'Yeah. You too.'

She looked towards Yanis.

He partially closed his eyes as he slowly nodded his instruction to her.

She bent down and tried to remove her shoes but the rope was too tight. She slumped, suspended in mid-air as she struggled to stand. Her face reddened as she began to choke. She looked fearfully at Harry. 'You don't mean for me to do this – do you?'

He sighed as he exhaled his impatience. 'Just do it. Stop wasting my fucking time.'

She removed her skirt and blouse and shivered as she stood in front of him in her grey bra and pants.

Harry turned his attention to Yanis. 'I said, strip. Everything!' He turned to Savina. 'How many times do I have to tell you? Come on.' He grinned. 'I want you both naked.' He tightened the rope as he walked towards Yanis and pushed the nozzle of the gun into his forehead. 'I said now. Both of you!' Harry shook with anger and wiped at his forehead with the back of his gloved hand. 'This is the last time I'll tell you.' He glanced towards the window and, for a split second as the lightning flashed across the sky, the anger in his face was gruesomely exaggerated. 'Just do it,' he raged.

They quivered as they removed the rest of their underwear and both tried to retain a semblance of modesty as they stood quivering in front of him. He pulled a cattle prodder from his rucksack and jabbed it into their buttocks.

While they screamed out in shock he tapped his hand on the backs of the two carver chairs and pushed them into them. He removed a large roll of silver duct tape, preferred by musicians, from his rucksack. He taped their wrists to the arms of the chairs and pulled the tape tight around their ankles, binding them together. After checking that they were unable to escape, he removed the noose.

CHAPTER TWENTY-THREE

Under Pressure

'So, tell me about the fire,' asked Harry.

'Fire?' mumbled Yanis.

'Come on. You know what I'm talking about.'

They both shook their heads frenetically.

He pulled a zippo lighter from his jacket pocket and moved towards Yanis. He flicked it into life and brushed at the Greek's hairy chest with his free gloved hand.

Yanis pulled back as far as he was able but Harry leaned across and burnt an area around his nipple.

The fat Greek screamed out as the foul smell of his singeing hair filled the air.

Harry clicked the lid of the lighter and held the closed Zippo in the palm of his hand. He leaned in to Yanis conspiratorially and their noses touched. 'Now tell me about the fire. Eh?'

Savina answered for her husband. 'Yes ... we did it,' she screamed.

Harry spun around and clicked back the lid of the lighter and flicked it into life. He separated her bare legs and held it within a few inches of her pubic hair. He watched the fear in her eyes. He enjoyed it. He closed the lighter and grinned at her before returning to Yanis. He smacked him around the head. 'You had to wait for your wife to tell me.' His gloved hand squeezed his victim's face until it looked as though his fat cheeks were about to explode. 'Why?' yelled Harry.

Yanis shook his head and mumbled unintelligible nonsense until he was able to speak coherently. 'Why the fuck did *you* do it?'

'Do what?' mouthed Harry as he released him.

'*You* helped them to escape,' yelled Savina.

Harry turned and glared at her. 'Escape from what?' He paced the room for a few seconds and returned to her. 'What the hell would they want to escape from?' He took his time to look around the luxury flat. 'Look at this place.'

Savina was adamant and repeated herself. 'You helped them to escape.' She paused and continued in a high pitched shriek. 'Why should you get away with helping them? They were ours –'

'You think you owned them?' yelled Harry. He balled his fists and bit at his lip, but didn't feel it. 'Like a pair of fucking dogs!' He kicked out at the third chair and it flew across the room, landing upside down beneath the table. 'They were *yours*?'

They both looked at him and nodded.

'Of course they were,' said Yanis, defiantly.

Harry grabbed at his own hair and tugged it. 'Hold on. Let's just rewind a minute.' He shook his head violently. 'So you're telling me ... they escaped?' He screwed up his face. 'But why would they want to do that?'

Silence.

Harry continued. 'So ... what did you do with them? Where are they now?'

Savina looked towards Yanis and continued. 'We don't know.' She turned to Harry. 'But we know ...' She scowled at him. 'You helped them –'

'Me?' He slapped his own forehead. 'I get it. You set fire to my place because you thought, I'd ... I'd ... I'd helped those two young girls ... to escape?'

'Yes,' snarled Savina.

'What? Are you both raving mad?' He reflected. 'I didn't.' He paused and fired questions at each of them, turning his head from side to side. 'So, where the hell are they now? What happened to them? How did they work for you? Tell me what you had them do?'

They both fidgeted nervously.

'Tell me ...' Harry dragged another carver chair from beneath the table and sat facing them. 'Why don't you tell me what happened?'

There was an uneasy silence.

'Listen.' He hammered on the arms of his chair. 'You may think I'm a fool but I am holding all the cards. Now tell me!'

Yanis offered Harry an intense shaking of his head. 'So you didn't help them?'

Harry made to stand. 'Did you really believe that? Is that what drove you to ruin my fucking life? Burn down my bar?'

Savina nodded slowly.

A look of sheer disbelief crossed Harry's face. 'Was Zavos in on it? Is that how you pulled it off?' he asked.

Silence.

Harry continued. 'Your tiny ... warped minds ... blamed me. So where the hell are they? Tell me about the girls.'

193

'Ah, the girls,' said Yanis, sarcastically.

'The lying is over.' Harry checked his watch. 'You've both run out of time,' said Harry.

Savina forced a smile. 'If we tell you … will you let us go?'

Harry snarled. 'What do you think?'

Yanis pushed out his tongue from behind his top bleeding lip and forced a vacant smile.

'What would you do?' asked Harry.

Savina grunted.

Yanis cleared his throat and yelled out. 'It was her idea,' he said, nudging his head in his wife's direction.

She grunted.

Yanis continued to spurt out excuses. 'The day after they arrived she drugged them. They were pretty and …' He took his time to remember them before he continued. 'And very good bodies,' he said, with a vile laugh.

Harry snorted as he tried to contain his anger.

Yanis continued. 'We knew they would make us a lot of money.'

Savina grinned and nodded. 'A lot of money,' she said.

Harry ignored her and turned to Yanis. 'Get on with it.'

Yanis struggled to breathe and began to hyperventilate. 'Each day we gave them more. At first, we put it in their drinks but after a week they realised something was wrong.' He grinned hideously. 'So we starved them until they couldn't walk, and she …' He nudged his head in the direction of his wife and continued. 'Injected the drugs into them and waited until they agreed to do whatever she wanted.'

Yanis looked across at Savina and cringed. 'She dyed their hair orange. *Bright* fucking orange …' He glared at his wife in disgust. 'Can you believe that? Then she painted their nails black – hands and fucking feet. They looked hideous.' He wrinkled his nose in disgust. 'Like whores,' he said.

Harry grunted.

Savina looked condescendingly at Harry. 'You almost caught us. They heard you when you and your prying fucking daughter came looking for them.'

Harry stiffened and made to get off his chair but thought better of it.

He waited.

Savina grinned. 'But an injection put them back to sle ... ee ... eep,' she said, extending the last word, dreamily.

Yanis continued. 'When they agreed to do whatever our clients wanted we fed them and put their pictures on the internet.' He smirked at Harry as he continued. 'And we waited –'

Savina interrupted him and shot him an arrogant smile. 'It didn't take very long.'

Harry growled. 'You bastards – that's beyond belief.' He tensed his fists in anger. 'Your horrific treatment of those two innocent young girls is ...? He snarled and kicked out at them. 'You treated them like animals – so you could both make money from their young bodies.'

Silence.

Harry could no longer control himself. He jumped up, grabbed his chair and swung it around his head before hurling it across the room. He grabbed Savina's handbag and pulled out the bundle of euro notes. He flicked the notes between his fingers and mentally counted them before pushing them into a pocket in his rucksack and securely closing the flap.

'How much of that did those girls earn for the two of you?'

'We helped them. They had nothing when you brought them to us –'

'Are you sure about that?'

Yanis and Savina looked at each other quizzically.

'What you did ...' Harry deliberated on his choice of words before he continued. 'Was fucking inhumane.' Harry rubbed at his chin. He took his time to walk towards Savina. When he reached her he forced the gun between her legs. 'How would you like it?'

She let out an ear-shattering scream.

Harry closed his eyes and exhaled.

Yanis struggled in vain and aimed his obscenities at Harry.

Harry ignored him. 'You'll both know soon enough,' he said. 'So when did they escape?'

'Two weeks before the fire,' spurted Yanis.

'You burnt me out that quick.' He stormed around the room kicking out at everything within his reach. He returned to them and continued. 'You did THAT, without knowing if it had anything to do with me?' He shook his head and roared his contempt. 'Who the hell do you so called *people* think you are?'

Savina looked at him and, lacking all emotion, she spoke. 'You caused us much embarrassment with our clients.'

'ME,' he roared. 'I caused *you* embarrassment. Is that what you call it?' He stormed out of the room and slammed the door behind him. He returned a few minutes later and, as he pulled a carrot and a cucumber from behind his back, he fired them a vulgar grin.

They frowned and as they shook their heads frenetically their dread was evident.

'What the hell is this all about, Harry?' asked Yanis.

'You'll see,' he said, while he busied himself with the rope.

He placed the noose around their necks, pulled it tight, and wrapped the other end of the rope around his hand. He cut through the duct tape and released them. He held the carrot and cucumber out in front of them. 'Choose one,' he roared.

They both shot him a confused look.

Reluctantly, they each reached out and made their choice.

Harry tugged the rope and as they both struggled to keep their balance he dragged them towards the settee and forced them to stand behind it.

He motioned to Yanis. 'Bend over.'

Yanis quivered as he partially bent over.

Harry glared at Savina. 'Do it.'

'What?'

'Shove it up his vile ass!'

She trembled as she moved the cucumber towards her naked husband.

Harry sneered at her. 'Do it … now.'

She grimaced as she pushed it into her husband's rectum.

Yanis tried to stifle a scream but failed.

'Further – all the way,' roared Harry.

She closed her eyes as she spoke. 'Sorry, love,' she said, softly.

Yanis screamed in agony as the cucumber pierced his colon.

Harry tugged at the rope and ordered him to stand up.

Yanis pleaded for mercy as he tried to stand.

Harry jerked the rope and turned his attention to Savina. 'Now you – bend over.'

She bent over the back of the settee and waited.

Harry looked at Yanis and waited. 'And now it's your turn.'

He grinned at him. 'And... *not* in *your* favourite place,' he ordered.

Yanis exuded sheer panic.

Harry grinned and spoke softly. 'Just do it.'

Every step Yanis took towards his wife delivered excruciating pain which shot through his whole body.

Harry tugged on the rope. 'Do it ... now!'

'Sorry,' said Yanis, as he pushed the carrot deep into his wife's anus.

She wanted to scream but retained her misplaced dignity by biting at her tongue. She could feel her mouth filling with blood. She held onto it until she was able to face Harry. She spat the blood directly at him. The blood was hardly visible as it ran down the already rain soaked black leathers before dripping onto the floor.

Harry tugged hard on the rope and they groaned as they struggled to breathe. He waited for all colour to drain from their faces before he finally released his grip and motioned to them to sit back on the chairs. They both screamed out in absolute agony as they reluctantly obeyed his orders.

He saw the hideous fear in their eyes.

Harry relished it.

He revisited his rucksack and took out a case containing a syringe and a small plastic phial of a drug he had originally planned to administer to Malik. The phial and syringe had been small enough for him to take through security at Bristol airport in his wash bag. When he showed them proof of his diabetes he passed without any further questions.

Now they could smell their fear.

'Is it necessary to do this, Harry?' asked Savina patronisingly.

'I'm afraid it is,' he said. He sneered at her. 'Surely you understand that?'

Savina tried to shrug her shoulders.

She failed.

Harry walked to the table and carefully picked up the syringe, filled it, and expressed a shot before making his way towards Yanis.

Yanis struggled again but Harry smacked him around the head for the second time. He initially slumped back but hung mid-air as the rope prevented him from falling to the floor.

Savina's mobile pinged.

Harry picked it up from the table and read it.

> Can we order a chicken pizza and pasta with
> extra cheese for tonight?
> Zavos & Achim

He read it again.

He looked at the names at the end of the message. 'What?' He reread it and looked up at Savina and Yanis. 'What's this about your pizza?' he asked.

They attempted to ignore him by turning their heads away.

Harry reflected on what Zavos had written in his message. 'Pizza? What is it with pizza? Why would Zavos and Kallidis want to order *that* from you?'

They ignored him.

Harry sensed they were hiding something. He grunted as he checked his watch. He then turned his attention to the mobile and sent his reply.

> **Ready for eight prompt**

CHAPTER TWENTY-FOUR

Thunder In My Heart

Harry forced Savina and Yanis to walk down the stairs and into the taverna. Every step raised painful and agonising yelps from them.

'Where?' asked Harry.

He sensed their reluctance to give him any clues but he saw them glance furtively at a door near the counter before turning away. As he tugged them violently across the bar they found it hard to keep their balance without excruciating pain firing throughout their bodies.

He tried the door.

It was locked.

'What is this?'

Yanis and Savina answered at the same time.

'Our cellar – where we store the food,' said Yanis

'A cold room,' blurted out Savina.

Harry mouthed to her. 'Cold room? Cellar? Open it!'

'We don't have a key,' said Savina.

'We lost it,' said Yanis.

Harry shot them an outlandish smile.

'Open it, I said.' He dragged them across to the counter and shortened the rope. 'Open it,' he said, as he tugged it, dragging their faces down onto the counter.

Yanis reached beneath the bar and attempted to hand the key to Harry.

'You unlock it,' said Harry.

Yanis didn't move.

'Now,' yapped Harry.

Yanis unlocked the door and passed the key to Harry. He slipped it into his jacket pocket.

As soon as the door opened Harry heard moaning and whimpering. He pushed Yanis and Savina through the door and down the stairs. The lights came on automatically and what Harry saw shook him to the very core. 'What the fuck? Is this for real?'

Yanis and Savina displayed no reaction.

When the occupants of the cages saw Yanis and Savina they cowered at the rear of their enclosures and lowered their heads submissively.

Harry recognised the young boy that had released Nyla in the warehouse more than twenty months earlier. Harry had a special regard for him and spoke to him in Arabic. 'Thank you,' he said. He paused and smiled at him before continuing in a soft voice. 'Sorry. I will help you.'

The young boy, who was no older than seven, forced a smile and then lowered his eyes. The girl in the next cage was more withdrawn; she was probably six years old and wore a filthy t-shirt and held her worn teddy bear tightly to her tiny malnourished frame. The end cage held a much younger boy who was wearing a filthy nappy. He had been a baby when Harry last saw him in the warehouse.

He turned to Savina. 'What happened to their mother?'

She looked at him with cold callous eyes and hissed. 'She died,' she said, defiantly.

Harry was lost for words and shook his head in total disbelief. 'You fucking people.'

The three cages were bolted to the black and white ceramic tiled floor and the occupants wallowed in their own urine and faeces. Three walls of their prison were covered with erotic pictures and photographs of naked babies surrounded by high denomination notes in various currencies. Insanely creepy artwork from Biljana Djurdjevic; boys and girls tied up and gross paintings of torture. There were also paintings from Marina Abramovic, with her spirit cooking, horns and blood covered skulls and headless people. In pride of place were horrific photographs, although at the first glance barely recognisable, of torturous acts being carried out on Nooda and Haya.

Harry closed his eyes and, as his whole body tensed with extreme anger, he tore into Savina and Yanis. While he beat them he looked up at the fourth wall. There were hooks and chains, horrific latex masks and numerous leather sado-masochistic paraphernalia, much of which Harry had never seen or could have imagined. He continued to transfer his anger to his prisoners and struck out until they begged him to stop.

He did.

While they lay semi-conscious Harry took his time to take in the room. He noticed there were three doors. He closed his eyes and recollected something he'd seen circulating on YouTube about restaurants in Washington DC, but had dismissed it as Fake News. Now he knew what had been going on in this basement.

He sighed deeply and spoke as he exhaled the shock. 'My God.' He talked to himself. 'You are so stupid, Harry. How did you miss that?'

Harry grabbed at his semi-conscious prisoners and lifted them onto the hooks on the wall, hanging them side by side. He grabbed at Yanis's arm, tapped the syringe and expressed it before jabbing the needle deep into it.

Savina screamed and Harry was left with no option but to take out a second roll of duct tape from his rucksack and press it across her mouth before pushing the refilled syringe into her arm. Within seconds they were both paralysed but able to hear and watch everything he did.

'The pair of you are worthless pieces of shit. Do you know that?'

They stared blankly ahead.

He lifted their heads and photographed each of them on their own mobiles and saved them to send to all of their contacts at a time of his choosing.

He decided to leave the children in the cages until his visitors arrived and after collecting food from the fridge up in the bar, he pushed it between the bars. While they gorged on the food Harry tried each of the three doors, dreading what he may find inside.

They were all locked.

Harry noticed there were cameras everywhere and soon traced the cables to one of the three doors. He thought for a few seconds and, while he looked around the room, he took his time to check each of the obscene picture frames on the wall. When he tapped at the side of the photograph of a naked hunchbacked woman, it slid open to reveal a row of unlabelled keys. He grabbed all of them and tried each door until he was able to unlock all three.

The first room had black and white ceramic floor tiles. The walls were decorated with bright red emulsion. Painted pentagrams and drawings of demons hung on each wall interspersed with many of the same pictures he'd seen in the other room, and more horrific latex masks, tools of torture and two beds separated by a garish striped curtain. There were more photographs of the three children and huge photographs of Nooda and Haya lying naked and being abused by naked men and women wearing grotesque animal masks and satanic robes.

The second room was very different. The floor was again tiled with black and white ceramic tiles. The walls and ceiling of the main room were painted black. In the centre of the room were two benches, each with leather straps at each corner and assorted torture equipment, various whips, a cat of nine tails and black leather studded masks. In pride of place were life-sized photographs of Nooda and Haya standing side by side, with their legs wide apart, emitting forced tortured smiles, and naked except for a slice of pizza covering their vaginas. At one end of the room was a clear glazed door that led to the black tiled wet room and bath.

The third room had a bank of video and DVD recorders. He looked at the multiple screens, fed by the cameras in all three rooms that covered every inch of the wall.

Harry checked his watch against his captive's mobile.

It read seven o'clock.

He had an hour.

He spent valuable time burning some of the depraved videos onto discs.

He had forty-five minutes left.

He walked back to the main room and tore the cable from every camera and smashed each of them in turn with a snooker cue that he'd seen being used as an instrument of torture in the videos. Whilst he held it firmly in his gloved hand, ideas came into his head of ways to use it to further torture his unwilling victims. He wiped those thoughts from his mind and, after placing the cue across his knee and breaking it in two, he prodded Yanis and Savina in the stomach before flinging the pieces across the room.

Ten minutes later he left by the rear door and locked it after him.

He returned at a quarter to eight. He dimmed the lights, left the rear door unlocked and the door to the cellar slightly ajar, before hiding behind a screen that divided the kitchen and the shelves stacked with tins and boxes.

At exactly 8:00 pm he heard a car pull up behind the taverna and two doors slam shut. The visitors arrived and pressed the intercom button four times.

Harry picked up the handset and replied in a muffled Greek voice. 'It's open. Come on down.'

He could hear their footsteps approaching the basement door. With excitement in every step, a voice called out. 'Yanis?'

There was no reply.

The only sounds that came from the basement were the children who cried out in fear of the visiting torturers.

The men smiled to each other before walking down the stairs.

Harry locked the rear door and turned off the taverna

lights. He entered the basement and slammed the door loudly behind him. Zavos and Achim looked up at the leather-clad, helmeted stranger standing at the top of the stairs. The stranger turned the key in the lock and slipped it into his jacket pocket. He pulled a gun and spoke in Greek. 'Hands in the air. Now!'

'What?' asked Zavos. 'Don't you know who I am?' he bawled.

The stranger spoke. 'I said, put up your filthy fucking greasy hands.'

Reluctantly they raised them.

Harry now took his time to study Zavos and Kallidis. They looked so different out of uniform. Their hair was greased tight to their heads and they both wore ripped denim jeans, trainers and black t-shirts with large suggestive motifs on the front.

Before they could argue, he rushed at them. He smashed the butt of the gun into their heads and they fell to the floor. He searched their pockets, removed their mobile phones, took the cash out of their wallets, and hurled the policemen across the room. When they slowly came round they shook the numbness out of their heads as they looked at each other. Terror slowly filled their ashen faces. Although they were naked they still made exaggerated and token attempts to cover their genitals but their wrists and ankles were fastened with cable ties.

Harry effortlessly hoisted them up the wall and chained them to the hooks next to Yanis and Savina and he took his time to remove his crash helmet.

The grotesque look on his captives faces exuded masks of utter confusion. Zavos was totally shocked and it took him several seconds to acknowledge what was happening. He finally summoned enough energy to speak. 'Harry,' he said. He closed his eyes and reopened them. 'You?'

'Yes, it's me,' he said, glibly.

Harry pushed his gun into Zavos's temple.

Zavos forced a smile. 'What are doing back here?' he asked, with a quivering and uncharacteristic, high pitched voice.

'Why do you think?' He pointed at Yanis and Savina. 'I came for them.'

Zavos turned to look at them and cursed under his breath.

Harry grinned. 'But look what I found.' He lashed out at each of the policemen. 'Did you all crawl out from under the same rock?'

Zavos forced a painful smile. 'Come on, Harry. How long have we known each other?'

Harry grinned at him and pushed himself up onto his toes. 'Listen to you … you filthy bastard.' He took a deep breath and, unable to control his anger, he pushed his nose into the inspector's face and screamed. 'We never really knew each other … did we?' Harry gritted his teeth. 'If I had any idea you were such a pervert, doing this evil shit, I would have killed you a long time ago.' He reflected. 'And it would have saved these poor kids …' He looked across at the confused children and continued. 'From your torturous and vile cravings: the sick debauchery and depravity.' He turned to Kallidis. 'You all betrayed innocent children. You made them victims – your sexual playthings,' he said, as he punched him repeatedly in the ribs. He returned to face Zavos. 'Did you set this up with Malik?'

He shot Harry a brazen look and grinned. 'Maybe,' he said.

'You all make me sick,' said Harry, extending every word as he remembered what vile depravity he'd seen on the computers.

He now turned his attention back to the whimpering Kallidis. 'How long have you been involved in this, eh?'

The policeman shook his head.

Silence.

Harry scratched his head and turned to Zavos. 'That night you arrested me ...' He paused. 'You bloody did it so he could grab the kids.' He nodded thoughtfully. 'You created another diversion.'

Zavos looked across at Kallidis.

Kallidis nodded as his fearful manner changed to bluster. 'Sure we did. How else could we have got hold of them?' he bragged. He smirked at Harry and licked his lips. 'It's hard to get a decent pizza on this island.'

Harry exhaled deeply before continuing to address Kallidis. 'But you didn't want their mother, right?'

'She was past her sell by date –'

'Did you kill her?'

Kallidis nodded. 'Sure we did.'

'Bastards,' raged Harry. 'If you're lucky, you may both live to regret it.'

Zavos smiled to Kallidis and they both grinned at Harry.

Kallidis said, 'Harry.' He sniffed. 'You may have forgotten that we are the police –'

'Police?'

'You won't get away with any of this, Harry,' said Zavos.

'You're so wrong,' said Harry, 'maybe I could talk to your people who were transferred to Larnaca?'

Zavos gave his response with a high-pitched scream.

CHAPTER TWENTY-FIVE

Hungry Eyes

Harry picked up their mobile phones, pointed them menacingly in their direction and clicked uncontrollably. 'When everyone sees your photos and what you've been doing to innocent kids and those girls.' He cursed. 'They won't give a damn who the hell you are. They'll see you ... for what you are ...' He took time to think. 'The most despicable and evil creatures ...' He had second thoughts. 'Animals!' He took a deep breath. 'The lowest of the fucking low. After this, I doubt you will ever be able to show your faces anywhere on the island and ...' He shook his head and grinned at them. 'I'll be surprised if you even make it to prison.' He grinned at them demonically. 'But if you do ... I doubt if either of you will ever get out of there alive.'

Harry stomped around the room like an enraged animal. He stopped suddenly and tugged a handful of black cable ties from his rucksack, wrapped them tightly around the three men's scrotums and tugged them tight. He then carefully selected three cables and plugs from the video room. He used his knife to strip each end of the cables and fit switches part way along before wrapping the bare wire around their contracted genitals. While he pushed the plugs into the nearest sockets, he talked to himself. 'Nah,' he said. Instead, he shook his head and then smacked his forehead with his free hand. 'That's too good for you.'

The tiny baby cried out and stopped almost immediately. Harry rushed towards the cage and smashed his way into it. He grabbed the now blue and unconscious little boy, laid him on the table, and in desperation administered CPR to his tiny malnourished body.

It was too late.

He retched as he picked up the dead baby and held him in his arms, before wrapping a large towel neatly around him and laying him on the table. He sat on the edge of the table and rested his left hand on the towel while he took his time to study the four tormentors. While he waited his anger built to a fit of utter rage. He turned away from them and as he clenched his fists his whole body trembled. Without warning he spun round and, with his eyes expressing his utter revulsion, he took his time to heighten their misery and suffering by stomping up and down in front of them like a man possessed. He suddenly stopped. 'What the hell is it with you … you … contemptible bastards?' His whole body shuddered. 'How come people can turn out like you? What would *your* mothers say if they saw you all now?' He picked up the dead baby and held it up in front of them. 'You did this … all of you!' His face contorted in disgust as he looked Zavos and Kallidis up and down. He gently placed the baby back on the table and, maintaining his stare on the children's oppressors, he removed the gun from his jacket pocket and took aim. He double tapped the Glock and fired two bullets into each of the policemen's knees. Their bodies bounced around as the bullets shattered their knee caps beyond repair. The shock produced streams of urine as the policemen pissed themselves. Harry was so angry he couldn't stop and, as the adrenaline pumped through his body, he doled out the same treatment to Yanis and Savina before sliding the smoking gun back into his pocket. He walked towards the wall and forced a switch into Zavos's hand and helped him to squeeze it. As the electricity pumped through his testicles and around his body, Kallidis pitched violently on the wall.

Harry, speaking in Arabic, asked the caged children if either of them wanted to flick the second switch to mete out the similar treatment to Zavos. The eldest boy, having suffered most since being incarcerated in the basement and fearful of retribution, shook his head. The little girl raised her hand tentatively, reached through the bars and grabbed blindly at the air. Harry nodded, took the cable and pushed the switch towards her. The young girl snatched it between her tiny fingers. Her grotesquely distorted face flashed with an unmitigated vengeance that Harry had never seen in anyone so young. She glared at all of them in turn and hissed her revenge. But in a bizarre twist, she fell silent and smiled mindlessly at Zavos as she flicked the switch. Simultaneously, Harry flicked the third switch and Yanis danced haplessly with Zavos.

While Yanis and Zavos screamed out in agony, their bodies twisted and jerked violently. Harry watched and waited until their bodies had stopped pulsating. He lowered his head and moved close in to Zavos. 'Did you know *they* burned down my bar?'

Zavos took his time to mock Harry. 'Of course I did,' he

slurred. 'I helped them do it.' His whole body shuddered as he continued in a laboured voice. 'It was unfortunate that the fire brigade were busy with a road accident outside of town.' He sniggered. 'A bad one – so I believe.' He smirked at Harry. 'But of course it turned out to be a false alarm.' He lied through gritted teeth and spat at Harry. 'Fucking tourists.'

Harry grabbed a piece of the broken snooker cue and thrust it deep into the inspector's fat hairy stomach and left it there.

Zavos urged and vomited blood.

Harry still wasn't satisfied. He returned to his rucksack, refilled the same syringe used on Savina and Yanis and walked towards Zavos. 'This is for the fire and …' He glared hard at Zavos. 'This will show you what your victims went through at your filthy hands,' he said, as he shook the syringe and released the air.

Zavos pleaded for mercy.

Harry ignored him and grinned idiotically as he stabbed the syringe into the inspector's naked thigh. He refilled the syringe and jabbed it into the chest of Kallidis. Within seconds they were both paralysed, unable to move and only able to see and hear what was happening around them. Harry took his time to take more photographs of each of them with their respective phones before waving the phones in front of them as he sent the pictures to all of their contacts. Satisfied with his efforts, he sighed heavily and took a deep breath.

He smiled at the children and spoke in Arabic as he walked towards the cages. 'Do you want to do anything else to these animals?' he asked.

There was no reaction.

Harry knew that all they wanted to do was to get out of their torturous internment so he picked them up and walked

slowly up the stairs. They were incredibly nervous and dis-
trustful, and hesitated as he put them down in the bar. He sat
them at a table and asked what they wanted to eat. They had
no idea so he made that decision for them. He took his time
cooking their food and sat with them while they ate in silence.
Although he spoke to them in Arabic, they didn't answer him,
instead they returned their appreciation with angst-ridden
smiles.

While they continued to eat, Harry pulled on his crash
helmet, unlocked Zavos's car and left his mobile, which con-
tained more incriminating photos he'd taken of those displayed around the walls, on the driver's seat. He then relocked
it and, after checking that the rear door to the bar was locked,
he walked along the quay to the only bar that was still open.

When Harry returned, the children had cleared their plates
and were sitting totally motionless at the table. He took them
to the flat upstairs and, while they were taking a bath and a
shower, he selected clothes that might remotely fit them and
ripped them to at least cover their tiny bodies. He stuffed the
wad of euros he'd taken from Savina's handbag into each of
their pockets and explained what was going to happen.

Carrying the knotted black bin liner containing the dead
baby, Harry walked them along the quayside towards the
lights of the restaurant.

He escorted them inside.

There was a small group of people sitting at a table well
away from the entrance. They looked up briefly but when
they saw the leather-clad stranger make a threatening move
towards them they returned to their drinks and nervous,
animated chatter.

When the owner of the Olive Tree saw the skeletal children troop in wearing the ill-fitting clothes, he looked uncomfortable and squirmed behind the bar demonstrating his reluctance to confirm his earlier arrangement with Harry. This changed as soon as Harry handed him five hundred euros. He immediately directed the children to a table with a view of the television fixed high on the wall behind the bar. The barman sat the children down, switched to the cartoon channel, and brought them drinks. Harry passed the bin liner to the barman. 'Give this to them when they come to collect the kids, OK?'

The barman nodded.

'And ... don't open it,' threatened Harry.

The children didn't want Harry to leave them but he managed to console them as he hugged each of them in turn before leaving. Harry was about to close the restaurant door when the little girl ran after him. She was hysterical. He helped her to calm down and finally understood that she had forgotten her teddy bear. He took her by the hand and walked back to the Harbour Side taverna. He left her sat at a table while he returned to the basement and pulled her teddy bear out of the cage. He looked up at Kallidis, Zavos, Savina and Yanis, and smirked. He entered the second room, carefully chose four suitable latex masks, and took his time to drag them across each of the deflated paedophiles faces. All they were able to do was watch him as he took one final look at them and spat in their direction.

CHAPTER TWENTY SIX

Rain and Tears

After taking the little girl back to the Olive Tree, Harry handed the empty Glock, with verifiable and albeit confusing evidence of Zavos's fingerprints on it, to the bar owner and left for the final time. He was full of trepidation as he closed the restaurant door behind him. He returned to the Harbour Side taverna, bolted the rear door, then made his way to the kitchen and turned on every ring and oven of the gas cooker. As he made his way to the front doors he took one final look around at the laid up tables and the part finished food, cups of coffee and tea, and the partially open basement door. He turned off all the lights except for a bank of three coloured lights inside the front doors, then locked the doors. He looked at the faded menu and photographs of pizzas hanging in the window. On the name sign above the taverna, he noticed the small logos; the pink heart and blue triangle that he'd seen on the Pizzagate website.

He shook his head and cursed to himself.

The gas hissed.

Harry called Nichole Mouzie from Yanis's mobile.

'Hello.'

'Hi, Nichole, it's me –'

'Harry?'

'Yeah.'

'I haven't heard from you for ages –'

'Fourteen months –'

'Is it that long?'

'Umm –'

'Where are you?'

'It doesn't matter where I am.'

'Are you in Paphos?'

'Listen.'

'Harry, what the hell is this all about?'

'There's a package at your office.'

'A package?'

'Yeah.' He sniffed. 'But it's not nice,' he said, as he thought about the gross acts he'd watched earlier.

'What?'

'Listen to me. You need to run with this.' He sighed heavily. 'Get it to your contact at Cyprus broadcasting, people at Sky and the BBC and email it to as many papers as you can and then load some of them up onto YouTube.'

'What the hell are you talking about, Harry?'

'You'll know when you've seen them. It's goes to the very top of Government and business in Cyprus.' He paused. 'Even further than that –'

'What?'

'Have you heard about ...' He paused. 'Pizzagate?'

'What the hell has pizza got to do with this?'

'You'll find out soon enough.' He took a huge breath. 'All

I ask is that you leave it twenty-four-hours and then send everything out to everyone in your little black book.'

There was silence.

'This is the story you've been waiting to write.'

She mumbled incoherently.

'Deal?'

'Yes. OK,' she said.

He could hear the doubt in her voice.

She exhaled and continued. 'Harry, what the hell have you done?'

He ignored her question.

'One last thing –'

'Yes?'

'There are two kids at the bar.'

Silence.

Harry continued in a reserved voice. 'Sorry, there are three, but one is a baby ...' He paused and sighed heavily. 'The baby's dead ... in the bin liner.'

'What the hell, Harry?'

He struggled to continue. He sniffed hard. 'Can you arrange ...' He coughed. 'To have him buried?'

'What is this all about, Harry?'

'You'll see. They're at the Olive Tree.'

She fell silent and he knew she wasn't sure where that was.

'The Olive Tree – a little way up from the Harbour Side taverna. It's the only one still open.'

'Ah, yeah. I know it,' she said, nodding to the invisible caller at the other end of the phone. 'What's that about, kids?'

'I want you to collect them and make sure they're looked after. They've been through hell.' He paused and lowered his voice. 'Worse than that,' he said, as he sniffed and swallowed.

'Much worse …' He took a breath and continued with a soft voice. 'You'll see.'

'Harry?'

'They've got money – lots of it. And make sure you use it to help them.' He contemplated on what he'd said. 'Get them to hospital first – for a check-up and then get them some decent clothes.'

'Harry, just tell me what the hell is going on?' pleaded Nichole. The desperation was clear in her voice. 'Can we meet, Harry?'

'No time now. Get that package …' He paused and exhaled. 'And when you watch them – the DVD's …' He shuffled nervously on the spot and rubbed his eyes before he continued. 'Be sure to sit down.' He closed his eyes and shook his head erratically. 'If you can … watch them all.' He coughed. 'I didn't,' he said, refusing to hide the total repugnance in his voice.

'Harry –'

'Be careful.'

He clicked the phone and tossed it into the sea.

The gas hissed.

Nichole drove to her office and picked up the sealed package from reception. She sat at her desk and opened it. There were three DVD's, a mobile phone and a thick wad of money which was too much for her to even try to count. She slid it across her desk. She flicked at the mobile and viewed the first photograph. She was so shocked that she dropped the mobile onto her desk. She pushed herself back into her chair and sighed heavily as she placed her hands across her eyes. 'I don't believe it.' She opened her eyes and looked towards the ceiling as she continued to talk to herself in an emotionally strained voice. 'Harry ...' She reached out for the mobile phone, flicked onto the next photograph and gasped in despair. After looking at two more of them she was totally drained and shocked beyond belief. 'Harry, what have they done?'

She pushed the money, DVD's and mobile phone into her handbag, grabbed her car keys and drove to the Olive Tree.

The gas hissed.

While Harry waited for Nichole to arrive at the Olive Tree, he re-entered his decimated dream and shone a fine beam of light from his torch, climbed over the debris, and made for his workshop. He tapped a stone in the wall to reveal his much larger, second fireproof safe door. He clicked the tumbler, reached inside, and removed the stolen L115A3, long range rifle, preferred by him and snipers in Afghanistan since 2008. The rifle, a .338 Lapua Magnum, also featured a sound suppressor and sights with improved magnification. He stripped it down in a few minutes, reassembled it, and made a few minor adjustments to the sights before pointing it at the wall and pulling the trigger.

He loaded it before walking back on to the breakwater.

He waited.

The gas hissed.

Harry saw Nichole arrive at the bar. The children rushed up to her and hugged her tight. 'It's alright,' she murmured, as she held back a tear. 'We'll take care of you now.' They hugged her even tighter. 'It's alright. You're safe now.'

She picked up the bin liner and gazed into space before looking out across the harbour towards Harry's decimated bar. She talked to herself. 'Thanks, Harry. But what the ... ?'

They didn't understand a word she said. But it didn't matter. They could feel her genuine love as she reciprocated with forceful hugs.

While the fork lightning lit up the whole harbour and thunder crashed overhead, Harry watched Nichole help the children into her Saab, put the bin liner in the boot, and drive away. He had already calculated the time between the lightning flashes and the rumbling thunder and knew when he would fire. He aligned the rifle sights, took aim, and waited. As Nichole's car turned the corner, and the thunder boomed overhead, three shots rang out in quick succession and the light bulbs inside the Harbour Side taverna shattered. There was a pause of a split second before the initial explosion reverberated across the harbour and the building burst into flames followed by several thunderous booms as the building disintegrated.

Harry was blown across the breakwater by the force of the first blast and as he picked himself up he screamed out uncontrollably. Still grinning, he brushed himself off and returned the rifle to its secret compartment. As he passed his burnt out bar, he reached across and grabbed a souvenir. He left the breakwater and, while the flames of the Harbour Side taverna raged behind him, he stopped on the deserted quayside and took one last look across at his bar, and what had once been the most enjoyable part of his new life. He briefly relived the sound of his noisy guests; the Greek music, the smell of Mama's wonderful cooking, and couples dancing cheek to cheek totally oblivious to everything going on around them.

He wiped at his tears, shook his head and, as the wailing of the fire and police sirens approached, he rode away.

*   *   *

When Harry was within a hundred yards of Malik's bungalow, he parked his motorbike. But when he reached the
bungalow he was surprised to see the light of the television
flashing through the shutters. He crept round to the back
garden and eased the window to the swimming pool pump
room. He picked up a crow bar and took his time to work on
the window before climbing inside.

Someone was waiting for him.

He aimed at Harry's crash helmet and smashed it.

Harry fell to the ground.

He feigned unconsciousness.

While his attacker went to find something to secure him,
Harry crawled across the floor and tripped out the intruder
alarm.

It saved Harry's life.

The high pitched metallic wailing filled every room of the
bungalow before it reached out shattering the peaceful evening silence of the village.

His attacker was taken unawares and panicked. After
squeezing his huge frame into the Opel Astra, an aged run-
around kept by Malik for emergencies, he accelerated out of
the drive.

Harry disabled the alarm and the silence returned once
more with little or no interest from the villagers. The crash
helmet had saved Harry from the impending torture and a
slow and certain death. He took a litre bottle of water from
the fridge and drank it all. Not wanting to leave any clues, he
smashed it into tiny pieces. He did a sweep of what was once
a luxury bungalow. Many of the ceilings had been ripped out
to allow the builders to install tracks throughout the property,
which ran from the main rooms to the bedroom and adapted

disabled bathroom. Malik had an electric hoist in his bedroom to lift him from his wheelchair into bed and similar hoists in the sitting room, wet room and toilet. The tracks enabled his two carers to move Malik from room to room and out into the garden, and the warm sunshine, with the minimum of effort. Harry checked Malik's room and found a small brown leather case. It was stuffed with mixed currencies; euros, pounds and dollars. Harry checked the lining of the case and found a photograph of him taken at his bar along with a small piece of paper and his London address. Harry shivered at the idea of Malik having sensitive information and wondered how he had got it, and more importantly why. He cursed as he checked his watch and stuffed the higher denomination notes into his jacket. He threw the remaining notes into the air before trashing the property to simulate a burglary.

He checked his watch once more and returned to the hire centre where he placed the motorbike in its original position and took a few minutes to select a new change of plain clothes. He retrieved his travel bag from beneath the boxes and damaged Kevlars, and placed the money in the false bottom. After placing his leathers, the latex gloves, cables ties, boots and crash helmet in a skip, he poured fuel over them and lit it. He repeatedly checked his watch as he watched everything burn. He reset the security alarm but chose not to reconnect the cameras. It stopped raining and as the full moon broke through the remaining clouds, reflecting its light from the wet road, he took a leisurely walk to the Kings Avenue Mall then a taxi to the airport.

CHAPTER TWENTY-SEVEN

Get Lucky

When Harry had landed in Cyprus earlier, using his third passport in order to reduce any suspicion, he paid the sixty-five euros in cash for his return ticket to Bristol. That guaranteed him a seat and enabled him to pass quickly through the airport without any problems. Three hours later when his plane flew over Paphos, he looked out of the window. Despite the best efforts of the fire brigade, and the port and marine police, the fire continued to rage at the Harbour Side taverna. Harry smiled with self-satisfaction as the gas fuelled, sky high flames continued to light up the whole of the area in and around the harbour.

Harry flew into Bristol airport and took the bus to Exeter, then drove home. The following morning he returned to work at Tavistock, as normal, to start the new week. When he left the police station that evening it was already dark and it had begun to snow. He drove out of the unusually quiet moorland town and onto the moor. He shook unexpectedly as he felt the release from his past surge through his tired body. He wanted to savour the moment for as long as he could and took his time to drive the next eight miles along the icy moorland road. As he drove up the lane leading to his isolated cottage he saw that all the lights in the cottage were on, illuminating the snow around it. He knew immediately something was wrong. When he renovated the cottage he installed timers so that the lights in the rooms came on intermittently to deter any potential burglar. But for some reason, tonight they were all lit.

He turned off the engine and lights and waited.

Within seconds he'd formulated a plan.

He pushed his bags of shopping into the footwell, pulled the torch from beneath his seat, and checked the lane for vehicle tracks and footprints.

There were neither.

It began to snow much heavier and his vision became blurred. He tipped his head backwards and let the snowflakes brush against his face. He minimised the beam of the torch and climbed over the gate and into the field that ran behind his cottage. He shook his head and wiped his face as he systematically followed the dry stone wall with his searching fingers, taking care not to touch the wool covered barbed wire that had been strung out to prevent the sheep from escaping into his garden and out onto the moor. He crouched low and without making a sound continued until he was within twenty feet of his garden.

He turned off the torch.

He watched and waited.

Suddenly there was only darkness.

Sliding one foot in front of the other, he glided the last few feet until he reached his garden. Again, he waited for a few minutes before he climbed the wall behind his shed and undid the padlock. He slipped inside and, after taking care to slide the rusting filing cabinet across the floor, he lifted the trap door. Although he was shivering, he smiled to himself as he was reunited with his dearest friend. He unwrapped the Heckler & Koch Mark 23 handgun, effortlessly stripped it down, in the dark, then tested and loaded it. He slipped it into his jacket pocket and took his time to return to his Land Rover. He flicked off the interior light and pushed it back a few yards. He climbed in, taking care to leave the driver's door open. He started the engine and drove slowly towards his darkened cottage. When he was within a few yards of the front door he slid off the seat and disappeared into the night.

He waited.

And waited.

Finally, he made his way around the cottage and peered cautiously through the sitting room window. The only light came from the last embers of the fire.

The rear door had been forced open so he was able to let himself in without making a sound. He took his time to check every inch of the cottage but strangely nothing had been disturbed or anything taken. While he repaired the rear door and fitted two additional bolts, he tried to work out what on the face of it seemed to be a pointless break in.

He thought hard and remembered giving his mother's address to Zavos before he left Cyprus, and when he moved to Devon he gave the London post office his forwarding address. He talked to himself. 'That bastard, Zavos, gave it to Malik.' He paused. 'He had a lot to answer for.' He sniggered. 'Well, he's done that now.'

He swept the cottage twice for bugs and cameras before he

remade the fire, boiled the kettle, made himself a coffee, sat down in the sitting room and skyped Nyla.

'Hello, Dad,' she said.

'Hi, love. How are you?'

'I'm fine,' she said. She shot him a confused look. 'But it's not Wednesday.'

'I know.' He took a sip, of his coffee. 'We're snowed in over here.'

'Are you?' She tried to imagine snow but had never seen it. 'I'll have a look online when we've finished.' She took her time and smiled at the camera. 'It's been terrible here too; we've had storms, heavy rain, thunder, and dreadful lightning.'

Harry waited.

Nyla continued. 'And all hell has broken out here.'

'Really?'

'Yeah.' She was surprised at Harry's muted reaction and paused. 'You know the Harbour Side taverna?'

Harry didn't reply.

'You know the place? Where we took Nooda and Haya to work?'

'I know it,' said Harry, as he lit a cigarette. 'So what happened?'

'There was a massive explosion and it's been totally destroyed. The police are saying the explosion could be due to a lightning strike.'

Harry turned away from the camera and grinned.

'You should see it. There's nothing left.'

'Wow. Is it really that bad?'

'It's been all over the television and in the papers.' She thought. 'I'll send you the link to the news site.'

'OK,' said Harry. He had already seen it on the internet but feigned all knowledge of it.

Nyla continued. 'Two people died but they haven't identified them yet and...' She paused to take a breath. 'There were two survivors –'

Harry flinched with disappointment. 'Do they know, who?'

'Yeah, that inspector that used to come to the bar.'

'Zavos?'

'Yeah, that's right ... and also Savina,' she said showing her approval.

Harry grunted.

Nyla continued. 'You know ... that rude woman. They're both in intensive care at the moment. They sound in a real bad way. People are saying they don't know if they will make it.'

Harry fought to hide his disappointment from the laptop camera by turning his head away and blowing a huge cloud of smoke towards the screen. 'Are you alright?'

'I'm fine,' she said, as she lowered her head. 'Oh.' She raised her voice. 'I nearly forgot –'

'Yeah.'

'That vile man from the warehouse ... You know ... the one I told you I saw last week.' She swallowed hard. 'Well ...' She couldn't hide her excitement and gulped for air. 'He was found dead in his car, this morning ... drowned in the sea ... with his chauffeur.'

Harry nodded and looked directly at the camera and forced a hint of concern. 'Really.' He hadn't expected them to be found so quickly and hid his surprise behind his hand.

Nyla continued. 'Yeah, a diver found them off Chlorakas

Beach.' She briefly dreamed. 'I love that place. Do you remember when we all went there swimming ... when we had our picnic?'

He nodded and smiled into the camera.

'Drowned eh?' He feigned concern. 'You just be careful and stay with your mother. Call me again on Wednesday. Bye, love.' He blew her a kiss and clicked his laptop.

He pinched at his bottom lip and talked to himself. 'So what the hell is it with the break in?' He sat back and rubbed at the blackened insignia from the coffee machine that he'd removed from the bar. 'It can't be *him* ... already.'

CHAPTER TWENTY-EIGHT

It's All Over Now

The following morning, after checking the windows and double-checking the door locks and bolts, Harry swept the new snow off the Land Rover and drove towards Tavistock. He was about to turn off the radio when the voice of the early morning local radio DJ subconsciously attracted his attention. 'That was *Hazard* by Richard Marx,' He faded out the record and continued in an annoyingly cheery voice. 'A very apt song for such a snowy February morning.' He coughed. 'And, take care all you drivers out there.' He tried to stifle a laugh but failed. 'A lot of thought goes into this show – we don't just throw it together,' he said, as he laughed into the microphone. 'Now, I've got a request for Harry Stryker Clark.'

Harry shivered and sat bolt upright in his seat and lowered his head towards the radio. He craned his neck as he listened intently.

The DJ continued. 'I don't know if that is your real name but ...' He paused. 'If you are listening on this cold snowy morning – Harry Stryker, this is for you.'

The DJ continued. 'Harry, or do they call you, Stryker?'

He paused and laughed to himself. 'Really.' He didn't hide the scepticism in his voice as he continued. 'Well, if you *are* listening on this cold snowy morning – whoever you are ...' He nodded to his female producer and continued to laugh. 'Your lucky friends in sunny Cyprus are wishing you a very happy birthday and ... have chosen this song.'

As the music faded out Harry screamed at the radio. 'It's not my birthday. It's not my birthday. I said ... IT'S NOT MY FUCKING BIRTHDAY!'

The intro of *Out of Time,* a hit for Chris Farlowe, back in the sixties, blasted out of the speakers. Harry hit out blindly with his right hand and killed the radio. He pushed himself deep into the frayed and threadbare seat and sat staring up at the skyline that was even more beautiful than the first time he saw it almost nine months earlier.

Harry took an early lunch break and walked to Dukes, a café inside the granite buildings and walled square that surrounded the panier market. The plastic tablecloths with olive green circles were complemented with Chinese paper lightshades and curtains of the same colour. It was usually a busy café and had a core of lonely and elderly regulars who came several times a week to spend time with each other but, due to the snowy weather, it was unusually deserted. He wanted time to think so he sat outside, in the cold, at a table beneath the canopy lined with cane baskets filled with brightly coloured pansies and ivy, which hung down from hooks fixed to the fascia. Although there was a large plastic crate near the door, filled with blankets and hot water bottles for use by their clients, Harry smirked preferring to ignore them. In an attempt to keep warm, he tapped the heels of his boots on the icy covered rough-hewn granite paving stones beneath his feet. He ordered a coffee, toast, and marmalade, and as he buttered the toast he tried to come to terms with the bogus birthday wishes. He looked around the snow covered square and, for the first time, noticed the standard olive trees in matching ceramic pots, positioned evenly between every fourth table of the café. Harry smiled to himself as he remembered how olive trees grew wild on the hills across Cyprus, while here in the Dartmoor town they were seen as something exotic and special.

The more he thought about the request on the radio the angrier he became. He repeated every word over and over until he finally talked to himself. 'I thought I tied up all the loose ends.' He closed his eyes and scratched at his chin. 'What the hell is happening now?'

Then he remembered seeing his mother's London address in Malik's bungalow.

He finished his toast and walked through the unusually quiet panier market but paid little attention to the numerous stallholders selling everything from fresh fruit and vegetables, cheese, pies, cold meats including second-hand CD's, DVD's and books, crockery, clothes and work boots. He walked between the stalls and out into the square. He noticed an art gallery in the far right-hand corner and headed towards it. Drawn to a wall of unusual framed pictures, he stood for a while looking through the window at the bright paintings. He entered the gallery and stood gazing at the large paintings by Rozanne Bell. The assistant removed her miniature dachshund from her lap and put him down on her warm seat. She told Harry that Rozanne was the UK's bestselling artist at the moment and achieved the unusual effect by overlaying

231

her paintings with a clear resin, giving them a bright ceramic appearance. Harry exhaled as he let his fingers flick through the notes in his pocket. After lengthy deliberation, he pointed at a large framed painting of a bright sunny scene, somewhere in the Mediterranean, with sail boats moored to the quayside. 'I'll have that one,' he said.

'Don't you want to know how much it is?' asked the young assistant.

He shook his head and pulled out a wad of Malik's euros and American dollars. He paused. 'I assume you'll take these?'

'No problem – but I'll need to call the bank to get the exchange rate.'

He pointed at the laptop on her desk. 'Just go online and get the latest exchange rate and I'll let you have five percent more –'

'OK,' she replied.

She fired up her laptop and, after double checking on several sites, she counted out the money.

Harry paid her twelve hundred euros and six hundred dollars and slipped what was left of Malik's money in his jacket pocket. 'I don't want a receipt,' he said.

She placed his money in a different section of the till and smiled at him. She measured the back of the frame, drilled into it and fixed hooks and tying chord before wrapping it in bubble wrap. 'There you go – all you need to do is hang it on the wall.'

Harry knew that whoever had checked over his cottage would make their move sometime soon but of course he didn't know when. He placed his painting on the armchair and set about fitting sash locks to the ground floor windows. After decid-

232

ing to sleep temporarily in the second bedroom, he loosened some of the floor boards in strategic places, also doorways and alternate stairs, so he would at least get a few seconds warning of any attack.

Harry poked at the fire, grabbed at the empty wicker log basket, tucked the gun in the back of his tracksuit bottoms, flicked his t-shirt over the top, and walked outside. He reached the log pile but as he bent down he was struck across the head. As he slumped unconscious in the deep snow his gun fell out of his tracksuit and slid away from him into the deep shadows.

Harry came round an hour later.

'Hello, Stryker,' said his attacker.

Harry grunted his response. He forced his eyes to partially open and found himself in his garden, tied to one of his dining chairs.

His grunt was met with a series of slaps around the head. Each time he could feel his teeth cutting into his lips and the inside of his mouth. His attacker checked the electric cables that he'd found in Harry's shed and, after restraining his hands behind his back, he tugged at the cable before wrapping it tightly around Harry's body, and finally his arms and legs.

Harry felt the snow beneath his bare feet and, while he shivered and tried to come to terms with what was happening, he was struck several more times across his face and head. He tried to tilt his head to lessen the blows, something he'd been taught early on in his training.

His attacker stood in front of him, his arms crossed commandingly while the kitchen light cast a grotesque veneer across his face.

Harry tried to focus on his attacker but the blows to his

head had affected his vision. He spat out the blood into the white virgin snow and scuffed his secured feet as he tried in vain to lift them off the ice and snow.

His attacker hit out at Harry once more before walking into the house.

Harry shivered and tried to comprehend what his attacker had planned for him.

There was a loud tap on the window which gained Harry's attention.

Harry strained to turn his head towards the window and saw Gassiev for the first time. The unshaven Russian smirked at him as he held up a mug of steaming coffee and a large chunk of cheese. He took a massive bite into it and opened his bulging mouth as he spoke to Harry in Russian. 'Sweet dreams, Stryker – sleep well.'

After plundering the fridge and gorging himself on Harry's food, he turned off the kitchen light.

Darkness.

Gassiev had learned to survive in extreme temperatures in Oymyakon, north-west of Tomtor in Siberia, an area that had the reputation of being the continually coldest inhabited place on Earth. So he was more than capable of surviving any length of time on Dartmoor, no matter how cold it was. It was Gassiev who had broken into Harry's cottage. He had no plans to steal anything or do any damage but he wanted to get a feel of the place, should he need to go in again; preferably when Harry was there, to surprise him at a time of his choosing. He made his home in the woods less than two hundred yards from Harry's cottage and built a hide beneath the thickest pine trees, protected from the worst of the heavy snow. He caught a ewe and, after breaking its neck, skinned it and used every part of the animal to sustain him while he waited.

When Gassiev received Malik's final text he made his plans for Stryker but was surprised that he had risked venturing into the guarded retreat. *He must have felt confident or crazy, thought Gassiev.* After the unexpected debacle at the bungalow, he decided to carry out Malik's final request sooner than he had planned. He anticipated that Harry would leave the island as soon as he'd accomplished what he'd come to do, so he waited near the airport. He knew Harry would feel invincible after his recent success and the last thing he would expect was for anyone to follow him to England. But he did just that and took the next flight.

Harry knew that he would probably freeze to death within less than twenty minutes so he tried self-hypnosis; something he had learned when he was first chosen for the Special Forces as part of his gruelling training many years earlier.

The light came on in the bathroom and then in Harry's bedroom and he imagined Gassiev lying in his bed wrapped up in the thick warm duvet.

Harry knew he had to control his temperature and once more tried to lower his rate of breathing and retain any heat he could at the core of his body. But as his body temperature dropped, his eyebrows, hair and scant clothes were soon coated with a thin layer of frost crystals. The cloud slowly cleared from the sky, a million stars shone, and, as the light from the full moon glistened on the snow, the temperature plunged to well below freezing.

A fox that Harry had been feeding for the past few months

came to investigate. He sniffed at his bare feet, lay down and nuzzled into them before disappearing into the night in search of his prey.

Harry talked to himself and tried to imagine the hot summer sun on his naked back in Cyprus but, as the lone owl hooted into the night, he slipped into unconsciousness.

At first light, the rooks resumed their loud cawing as they dived amongst the trees and up into the sky creating weird shadows on the snow. Although the sun had begun to rise and pass slowly across Harry's face it had no effect on the ice that now swathed his whole body.

The bedroom light came on casting eerie shapes across the rest of the rear garden. Seconds later Gassiev walked into the kitchen and looked out at his frozen captive. He chuckled to himself as he boiled the kettle and made himself a coffee. He took a packet of sealed ham from the fridge, ripped it open, and pushed all of it into his huge gaping mouth. He took a massive slug of coffee and while it was still in his mouth he walked out into the garden and poked at Harry before kicking out at the chair.

As Harry fell into the snow there was a click and a blast from a gun. Gassiev grabbed at his chest and, as he fell to the ground, several more shots struck his body in quick succession. The rooks took fright and cawed fearfully as they flew out of the trees rocketing up into the clear blue sky and out across the moor.

CHAPTER TWENTY-NINE

Angels

Harry was blinded by the bright heavenly light and, as the warmth swept across his face, he could hear spiritual music and the voices of angels. He partially opened his eyes to look for them but instead saw the calm, blue azure sea. He pushed his toes into the pebbles and the waves lapped around his feet.

'Relax,' said the soft angelic voice.

He did just that and exhaled slowly.

The warm soft cloth gently wiped his eyes and mouth and then his whole face. He opened his eyes a fraction but the bright light blinded him. As the low sun moved across the wintry sky and away from the window, his eyes slowly became accustomed to the light. He noticed the ice on the outside of the window and a vase of freshly picked daffodils on the mantlepiece and, when he felt the warmth on his face from the fire burning in his bedroom grate, he fell back into a deep sleep.

It was several more days before Harry's body had warmed up sufficiently for his heart, kidneys, liver and lungs to function properly. He tried to speak coherently but was unable to do so; instead, he took his time to focus.

What he saw shocked him. 'You?' he groaned.

Silence.

Harry struggled with every letter and slurred. 'Where is he?' He coughed and his whole body shuddered. 'What happened to him?'

'He's dead,' replied the soft voice. 'You have a guardian angel – for sure.'

'Thank God, you've found me,' he said, continuing to slur each word as it exited his cracked and swollen lips.

Silence.

'How?' he asked.

'It doesn't matter at the moment. You were unconscious and freezing to death,' said the tender voice. 'You were very ill.' She held up his small bottle of morphine tablets and tapped it. 'We gave you these to help the pain. Was that, OK?'

Harry tried to smile but failed.

He had weaned himself off morphine when he returned to England but now he could well be hooked once more.

'To let you die out there ...' She glanced towards the window and after turning back to gaze at him, she continued in a stern voice. 'Was too easy.'

Harry tried to make sense of what she'd just said but was too sick to take anything in.

Nooda said, 'We saw the Russian and we waited for him to come inside and go to bed.' She spat symbolically and looked at Harry. 'He visited the basement with the other ...' She was lost for words but, after clenching her fists and shaking them in mid-air, she continued in Arabic. 'لي افلذن.' She opened her hands and covered her face then spoke through

238

her outstretched fingers. 'We wanted to kill him, so badly ... and ...' She struggled to continue but broke down.

Haya looked down at Harry and her pretty face slowly twisted into an inane grin. 'By the way, you lost a finger and a toe with the frostbite,' she said, flippantly.

Harry tried to move his arms but they were tied at the wrist. He shot the girls a bewildered look before he turned his attention to his bandaged hands and tried to wriggle his fingers.

He couldn't.

Nooda spoke slowly, 'Why did you sell us, Harry?'

He tried to make sense of her question but couldn't. He swallowed hard and spoke in little more than a whisper. 'What?' He could feel they weren't ready to answer him so he returned to thinking about his damaged limbs.

He shook his bandaged hands at them and blinked wildly. 'Which ones?' he asked.

Nooda tried to explain but didn't know the English word so she pointed to the ring finger on her left hand and wiggled it with the thumb and forefinger of her right hand. 'This one – but only to there ...' She straightened her finger, touched the lower knuckle and wiggled it. 'So you will still be able to use it for something,' she said. 'Oh ... and the little toe on your right foot.'

'How did you know what to do?' he asked.

'Come on, Harry.' Nooda wiped at her tears and smiled briefly. 'You have forgotten we lived through the hell of Aleppo and saw so much injury and death ... every day –'

'We helped to treat injured and dying people ... our friends and neighbours,' said Haya.

'Tell us, Harry, you have so many terrible scars on your body. What happened?'

Harry closed his eyes as he relived the experience. 'Do you remember when you were in the warehouse with Malik?'

They nodded.

'We didn't understand English then but we seemed to understand some of it because of your angry voice,' said Haya.

Harry continued. 'Well, Malik was responsible for what happened to me and then … Gassiev,' He tried to choke back the emotion. He continued. 'The Shadow.' He tried to wipe his eyes but the tears ran down his cheeks onto the pillow. Haya wiped them with a tissue. 'I was with Malik in Iraq.' Harry tried to laugh but managed little more than a squeak. 'Would you believe – helping them?' He managed to take a shallow breath. 'He shot me and thought he'd killed me but I survived. But then …' He swallowed hard as he remembered that day. 'The Shadow, that bastard, Gassiev …' He gulped in air and continued. 'He tried to finish it with an M67 – a hand grenade.' He gritted his teeth and swallowed. 'I was so lucky.' He nodded and closed his eyes. 'The medics took out my spleen and one kidney, part of my liver and fused some of my spine together. They put metal plates in my legs, shoulders and arms.' He smiled at them. 'But, do you know what?

'What?' they mouthed.

Harry gave them the broadest of painful smiles. 'I'm still alive.'

'Now we understand why you hated him so much,' said Haya.

'More than you'll ever know,' replied Harry.

Nooda and Haya looked at each other. 'We're sorry,' said Nooda.

Harry waved their pity away. 'So how did I get to survive that freezing …' He swallowed hard. 'Cold?'

Nooda said, 'On that night when you were tied up by the Russian.' She looked to Haya and smiled. 'I mean the shadow ...'

Haya continued, 'As soon as we knew it was safe we wrapped you in blankets and the old dirty white painty sheets we found in the shed, and then covered you with a big plastic sheet.'

'It kept you alive through the night,' said Nooda.

Harry tried to shake his head in total disbelief but it hurt. He failed.

'As soon as we saw the light come on in your bedroom window, in the morning, we removed everything and waited,' said Nooda.

'We found your gun in the snow,' said Haya.

Harry nodded. 'Hmm ... So what have you done with Gassiev?'

'We could not bury him because the garden was still frozen and too hard, so we emptied the large container of water at the side of the cottage and pushed him into it,' said Nooda.

'He was very heavy and he's still in there,' said Haya proudly.

'We're waiting for the frost to leave,' said Nooda.

Harry nodded his approval. 'Clever.' He was short of breath and struggled to continue. 'So, why did you help me ... and then tie me up?' He finally managed to lift his secured arms a few inches from the bed.

'*We* wanted you to kill you – so we were determined to keep you alive,' said Haya.

Harry blinked.

Nooda repeated her earlier question. 'Why did you sell us to *them* ... uh?'

'What? I don't understand,' replied Harry.

They both wanted revenge and they looked at him with unmitigated anger and hatred in their eyes.

Harry coughed violently and felt the blood filling his mouth. He swallowed it and wiped clumsily at his mouth with his bandaged hand, before speaking. 'Is that why you came to England?'

Nooda spoke divisively, 'Yes. To find *you* –'

'And kill you,' said Haya, firmly. She moved as close to him as she dared, pulled out his gun and pointed it towards his chest.

He sucked at his dry, split lips and then rolled them between each other. 'Come on … you know I had nothing to do with it.' He gasped. 'Do you really believe that?'

They looked at each other and spoke as they nodded. 'Yes … we think you did.'

Harry trembled with frustration. 'For God's sake,' he said. *He wasn't afraid to die but didn't want to die today, killed, by a young girl.* He continued. 'You're both a similar age to Nyla.' He gulped for air and exhaled noisily. 'Please don't think I would ever allow anything like that to happen to you … or anyone.' He shook his head. 'I just didn't realise,' he said, his voice fading.

Their dark eyes were more affable and for the first time he sensed their doubt.

'Look. What I can say, is that none of them –'

'None?' asked Nooda.

'Them?' asked Haya.

Harry held his painful grin for a while before speaking as he exhaled. 'That's right, none of them.' They looked at him and waited. He continued. 'Yanis, Savina, Zavos and that bastard Kallidis … all of them.' His body collapsed with exhaustion. He took his time to refill his damaged lungs before he continued. 'If any of them do survive, after what happened to them …'

'Did you do something to them?' they both asked wide-eyed.

Harry nodded. 'Yes, I did.' He tried to take a huge breath but failed. Instead, he coughed violently. He wiped the blood from his lips with the bloodied bandaged hand. He took another breath and sighed. 'They will spend the rest of their lives in purgatory.'

The girls looked at him for an explanation.

'They will suffer in prison and …' He forced a painful smile. 'Probably get murdered by the other prisoners … for what they've done.'

The girls looked disappointed that some of their vile tormentors were still alive and would go to prison.

Harry continued. 'That is if any of them do survive.'

They didn't understand and fired each other a questioning look.

Harry continued. 'You know what? I thought about Savina and Yanis and I guessed they had inside help – from the police. That's where Zavos and Kallidis came in. They had the authority to manipulate the situation, and people, to satisfy …' He reflected. 'To quench their vile needs.' He grunted his anger. 'Come on … untie me.' He lifted his heavily bandaged hands and looked at them forlornly. 'How can I go anywhere like this?'

They wanted to do it but they held each other back.

CHAPTER THIRTY

The Final Countdown

While Harry lay in bed wrapped tightly in his thick duvet he watched Nooda and Haya as they meticulously dusted the bedroom. He coughed to gain their attention and when they eventually looked at him he tapped the bed and motioned to them to sit on it.

'Listen, it's over,' he said. 'Malik is dead and now the Russian. I know you've both been through hell, and I'm truly sorry.' He lowered his head compassionately and closed his eyes. 'But this is the time for you to decide what you want now.' He opened his eyes and took his time to look at each of them in turn. 'I'll help you if I can, but my life is very different here and I don't honestly believe I'll ever be going back to the island.' He sniffed and forced a smile. 'Nyla may come here when she's finished college and go to university … maybe in Exeter.' He made an attempt to raise his shoulders but only achieved the notional raising of one of them. 'I don't know.'

The girls looked at him. *He was lost and exhausted; a shadow of the man who was full of energy and once ran the successful bar, Harry's Bar, in Cyprus.*

Nooda slipped the gun into her jacket pocket.

Haya released his hands. 'OK, Harry. We have discussed everything and we believe you.'

Harry closed his eyes and exhaled with relief.

They manhandled him down the stairs and into the sitting room. They helped him onto the settee in front of the log fire and wrapped him in blankets.

While Haya made coffee, Nooda placed a few of the smaller logs onto the fire and turned to face Harry. She picked up the scissors and paused. She was still not totally convinced of Harry's innocence and looked him in the eye for a brief moment until she felt sure. She cut off the cable tying his hands together and carefully checked his blackened fingernails, ears, hands and feet before removing the loose skin, cleaning the wounds and bandaging them again.

Haya handed Harry his coffee.

He held the mug awkwardly in his bandaged hands and sipped at it, but as the hot liquid seeped into the deep lacerations in his mouth he pulled back in pain. Haya rushed to the kitchen and returned with a straw. She slid one end in the coffee and the other end into Harry's mouth. As he sipped at it, she smiled at him. He grinned back at her. After drinking much of the coffee he slid the mug onto the table and slumped back awkwardly. Through his partially closed eyes, he looked at the wall above the fireplace. On it was the painting by Rozanne Bell that he'd bought at the art gallery the day Gassiev arrived to kill him.

He smiled to himself and closed his eyes. *Malik you bastard – you paid for that.*

Haya propped up his head with a cushion and he fell asleep.

*   *   *

Harry stirred and Haya looked down at him. 'Harry.' She lowered her voice to little more than a whisper and continued. 'We've eaten all your food ...'

'Who cares,' he said, with a smile.

Nooda smiled at him with pride. 'We used the internet and ordered a delivery –'

'Delivery?'

'Yes, we used your credit card ...' She smiled at him. 'And we got points too.'

Haya said. 'You ought to try it, Harry. It's great.'

Harry grunted.

He fell asleep briefly but was woken by the girls who were watching children's television and laughing excitedly. He had a question for them but while he waited he checked out the room.

It was spotless and warm.

How he imagined it might look and feel when he first moved in.

It was perfect.

When the programme finished he licked his dry lips and took a while to catch his breath before speaking. 'Tell me, how the hell did you both manage to escape?'

'One of our clients,' said Haya. 'He honestly ...' She paused and spoke as though she didn't believe it herself. 'He really ... liked us.' She smiled at Harry as though it wasn't possible. She wiped at her eyes and spoke in little more than a whisper. 'He did.'

'And why not?' muttered Harry.

Nooda touched Haya gently on her arm and spoke. 'And he arranged for us to get away ... while his friend took *them* to dinner.'

Nooda smiled for the first time. 'It was very lucky for us that we hid our passports and the money in the flat the day we arrived with you.'

'And we kept some tips from our clients,' said Haya.

Nooda gagged. 'Filthy bastards,' she said, 'I'll never trust any man … ever again.'

Harry lowered his head and sighed. 'In time you will,' he said. He took his time to raise his head and look directly at them. He smiled. 'We're not all bad.'

'Really?'

'It will take time,' he said. He nodded sympathetically. 'Just give it time.' He knew he had lied as he recalled all too vividly the foul and unspeakable videos and photographs he'd seen of them in the basement.

'Why did you go back after escaping the first time?'

'We needed our passports,' said Haya. 'We were trapped on the island without them.'

'So we had to go back.' Nooda grinned. 'The second time we made sure we had them … and our money … and we waited to escape.'

'He helped us the second time and –'

'Here we are,' said Nooda.

Haya looked at Harry and tilted her head suspiciously. 'Do you know sometimes we could hear you talking to them?'

'But not in detail,' said Nooda. 'That is why we believed you sold us to them …'

'Surely you know I would never do that, right?'

They both nodded and a smile slowly crossed their faces. 'Now we do.'

Harry nodded. 'So how did you find me?' he asked.

Nooda said. 'We texted Nyla and said we wanted your

address to send you a Christmas card.'

Haya giggled. 'And she gave it to us,' she said proudly.

'She knows you're both alright.'

They nodded.

'We said we were back in Syria,' said Haya.

Harry nodded. 'So how did you get here?'

Nooda said, 'By plane to Exeter.' She smiled proudly. 'At first, we stayed at a hostel in Plymouth and when we heard the request on the local radio –'

'Why were you listening to that crap?' asked Harry.

Nooda shook her head dismissively. 'We want to learn English, Harry, so we listen to the BBC local radio and watch television –'

'We love EastEnders,' said Haya.

Nooda continued. 'When we heard your birthday request we guessed that one of Malik's men had found you too.'

'Why,' asked Harry.

'Nyla told us your birthday is in June – so we knew it was not true. It was a trick or a joke.'

'We thought we could, as you English say, "kill two birds with one stone."'

Harry grunted.

'We found this house on Google maps and once we knew where you lived we took our sleeping bags and some food and asked a farmer in Tavistock to bring us to here,' said Haya, with a smile.

'She was very nice,' said Nooda. 'She is a sheep farmer.'

'We slept in your Land Rover.' She thought. 'Maybe you should lock it next time –'

'Maybe I will,' said Harry. He smiled as he tilted his head

back. 'Now we have to get rid of that Russian pig.' He thought deeply. 'I have an idea.'

That afternoon they ran Harry his first bath in many weeks and helped him up the stairs. Every few hours the girls replaced his hot water bottles, and he slept soundly for another three days.

CHAPTER THIRTY-ONE

Unfair Weather Friend

Two weeks later Harry sat unaided on the edge of his bed and looked out of the bedroom window at the moor that was still covered in a thick blanket of snow. A carrion crow flew down and ripped at the sheepskin left in the garden by Gassiev. He smiled as he watched a redwing gorging itself on the holly berries in his garden and at the rooks as they continued to swoop between the bare trees and up into the sky, fighting over their territory before finding a mate and nesting. He noticed the change in wind direction, the thickening clouds, and the mist obscuring the far off tor. He opened the window and, for a few minutes, felt the sun on his face.

Harry closed the window and called out to the girls. 'The weather is about to change and it looks like rain.' He sighed. 'We need to get rid of our unwanted guest today or it may be too late.'

Harry started the Land Rover for the first time in many weeks and, after several attempts of crunching the gear box, he slipped it into reverse, drove into the back garden and pulled up close to the shed. The girls helped him drag two scaffold boards from the shed and, after opening the rear door of the Land Rover, they made a ramp into the snow. They tipped the water butt on its side, rolled it towards the boards, and pushed it up into the vehicle. Harry grabbed the wrecking bar and axe in the corner of his shed and slid them beside the scaffold boards. He dipped the clutch and drove out of the garden and along the icy path towards the woods. When he reached the bog at the edge of the woods he reversed towards it, checking his position every few feet. He knew that if he drove too far they would be trapped and there would be no way they could get the vehicle out. He left the engine running and opened the rear door and remade the ramp with the scaffold boards. They let the water butt slide down the ramp and across the snow and ice. Harry then picked up the boards and slid them across the ice. They upturned the barrel and, after hitting out at it with the wrecking bar and back edge of the axe, Gassiev's contorted naked body slid out onto the snow.

Harry looked down at it and, for the first time, saw the tattoos that covered much of his body. Harry raised his head and looked towards the girls.

Nooda blushed as she spoke. 'We removed his clothes and burnt them –'

'He could be recognised if we didn't,' said Haya.

Harry grunted and then grinned at them. 'Good girls,' he said. 'You're learning much too quickly.' He paused. 'But the tattoos would be a giveaway, right?'

They thought for a second and then grinned back at him. 'Yes, of course. We could remove them,' said Nooda. She paused and grinned at him. 'I mean ... to take off the skin that has the tattoos.'

Harry laughed loudly and shook his head. 'No, we don't need to go that far.'

The girls hid their embarrassment by busying themselves. They grabbed a length of the electric cable used to tie up Harry many weeks earlier, wrapping it around the Russian's waist before pulling it up under his arms.

Nooda and Haya each stood on a board. They pulled the cable as they edged their way towards the end of them and dragged the body to the area already marked by Harry with twigs and broken branches. When they reached the carefully chosen spot they edged their way slowly back along the boards and Harry, with the help of the wrecking bar as support, made his way along until he reached the end. He then proceeded to smash at the ice with the wrecking bar and axe until he broke through it. He tugged at the cable and as it slid free from the body he pulled it towards him and wrapped it around his left arm before throwing it to Haya. He pulled his gun from his jacket pocket and, after checking it was loaded, he turned to the girls.

They shrank back in abject horror.

Harry smiled at them. 'Listen, I've already told you not to be frightened of me.'

They both forced a half smile but continued to slide their feet back towards the vehicle.

Harry reached awkwardly into his other jacket pocket with his bandaged hand and took out the suppressor. It took him several attempts to screw it into the gun but he finally succeeded with a grunt. He pointed towards Gassiev's body and shot a circle in the ice around it, until the gun clicked, empty. He slid the gun across to Nooda and she picked it up. He grabbed the wrecking bar and beat around the perimeter of the circle of ice but slipped and fell onto one knee, exhausted. He swore loudly and, after psyching himself up, summoned all his strength and pulled himself up on the metal bar. He took a huge breath and continued like a crazed person until the ice cracked and the circle rocked. He pushed at it and, as it tilted, Gassiev's body slid off.

They stood and watched as the dead Russian sank slowly into the green, muddy water. His huge body was immediately consumed by the bog. Within a few minutes all that remained were a few bubbles. The ice circle stopped rocking and refilled the gap.

Harry made his way slowly back along the planks. As soon as they were loaded in the Land Rover, he drove back to the cottage where he lay exhausted on the settee. He closed his eyes and revelled in the moment, knowing that he had got rid of his nemesis once and for all.

A few hours later the south westerly wind picked up to gale force and it rained torrentially. Heavy rain lashed the cottage for almost a week. While the fire roared inside, Harry showed the girls how to toast marshmallows on the fire on the long kitchen fork. After eating the whole bag of marshmallows, the three of them sat around the fire and reminisced.

Nooda looked at Harry and spoke in a stern voice. 'You have a lot of demons, Harry.'

Harry sucked hard. 'I know ... they won't leave me alone.' He looked at them with sorrowful eyes. 'Believe me, I've tried.'

'Can I ask one question, Harry?' asked Haya.

'Of course,' he replied.

'I know you lost your restaurant in the fire in Cyprus and I think at that time you were broke, yes?'

Harry nodded his reply.

Haya looked around the room. 'This is a lovely cottage but …'

'Go on, you can ask it.'

'Well.' She blushed. 'Where did you have the money to buy such a beautiful place?'

Harry smiled and then looked despondent as he spoke. 'My mother died when I came back from Cyprus –'

'I'm sorry,' said Haya.

'It's alright,' said Harry softly. 'She was ill and when my father died she had nothing to live for. I was in the army and hardly ever saw either of them in those twenty years.'

They looked at him strangely.

'I wrote to them,' said Harry, regretfully.

They both smiled. 'Ah,' they said, thoughtfully.

Harry continued. 'My mother was lonely … very lonely.' He sniffed. 'I wanted to stay in London but after she died … I couldn't stand the big city after living in Cyprus, so I came here and …' He took a breath. 'By chance, I found this place – it was a wreck.'

They didn't understand.

Harry smiled. 'It was badly damaged and in a terrible condition but I liked that. I could do what I wanted.' He looked around. 'And this is the result.'

'Yes, it's beautiful,' they said.

Harry looked concerned. 'Don't be fooled by the beauty. You mustn't forget that the moor is very mysterious and can be deadly dangerous. The fog and mists come down without any warning and you have no idea where you are. That's why they built the prison.'

They pulled back in shock and mouthed the last word.

'As I said – don't be deceived. It really is very dangerous.' He grinned. 'And there are bogs everywhere – animals and people can disappear forever – without trace.'

They both put their forefingers to their lips and smiled knowingly at him.

Harry raised the same blackened finger, put it to his lips, and nodded slowly. 'When the farmer showed me around the cottage; the garden, the huge woods and the stream ...' He grinned. 'And the bog, I couldn't believe what I was getting for the money.' Harry reached out, slid another log on the fire, and sat back. 'I never, ever, knew I would have a use for that.' He sucked at his lip. 'Now it's my turn.' He looked directly at them. 'So what are you going to do now?' He adjusted his cushion and waited for their response.

There wasn't one.

Harry continued. 'Now you have your passports, and money, you're free to go and work wherever you want.'

'We want to stay here – in the cottage.'

Harry rubbed at his damaged finger. 'I know what you mean. Who wants to be part of all the evil in the world, out there?' He paused. 'But none of us have that choice... you know we'll all have to re-join the madness very soon.'

'We know,' said Nooda sadly.

'We're going to work here,' said Haya, in a matter of fact way.

'Here?'

'Yeah.'

They looked at each other and grinned. 'We said we like it here ... and we will be training as nurses at Tavistock Hospital,' said Haya.

'We will have our own rooms too,' said Nooda.

'When do you start?'

'At the beginning of next month,' said Haya.

'We train for six months and then if we are good at the job … we will stay,' said Nooda.

'So you will see a lot of us from now on, Harry.'

'I'll like that.'

A car horn sounded outside and Harry looked up and fired them a puzzled look.

Haya left the room and when she returned she was wearing one of Harry's jackets, which was much too big for her.

Harry was shocked. 'What's going on?' he asked.

Nooda smiled at him. 'It's alright, the sheep lady is taking Haya into Tavistock to buy bread and milk and other shopping things.'

Haya smiled proudly. 'We'll be back in a couple of hours.' She looked across at Nooda. 'She will make your lunch.'

Nooda smiled at Harry who still didn't understand what the hell was going on.

'See you,' said Haya, from behind the door.

She darted out of the door and rushed to the shiny four wheel drive.

Nooda carried in a tray with sandwiches and mugs of steaming coffee and placed them on the coffee table in front of the fire. 'I've had a thought.'

'Yeah?'

'What about your job?'

Harry grunted and screwed up his face. 'I don't know – maybe another new start.' He seemed unconcerned and picked up his sandwich.

*   *   *

After the week of torrential rain, the sun finally came out once more and the transformation outside was incredible. The stream on one side of the cottage, that was once little more than a trickle, was now a raging torrent of muddy water racing down towards the Dart and out to sea. The front cottage garden, separated from the lane by the rich copper coloured beech hedge, was peppered with splashes of colour from primroses, snowdrops, crocus and daffodils. All of these were a total surprise to Harry as he spent his first winter in the cottage. Out across the moor, individual trees, stripped of their leaves months earlier, now stood skeletal and statuesque. As the sun passed across the moor it broke through the speeding clouds and revealed the beautiful moorland colours; the long tufts of last year's yellowing moor grass, peppered with clumps of purple heather, the yellow flowers on the windswept and disfigured dark green gorse, ferns and bracken. Spike rushes protruding from the bog and wetter areas, were all emphasised by the backdrop of the multi-coloured granite of the tors and the lower rocky outcrops.

While the girls were having a shower and getting ready for bed, Harry dimmed the lights in the lounge and skyped Nyla.

'Hi, Dad, where have you been? I've been worried about you. I've been trying to get through to you for weeks –'

'It's alright, love,' he said softly, as he tried to reassure her.

'Dad, I can hardly see you. What's happened? What's up with your camera?'

'Nothing. A couple of light bulbs have blown and I need to go into Tavistock to buy new ones. That's all,' he lied.

'So *where* have you been? It's been *weeks*,' she shrieked.

'I got caught in the snow that's all … had a bit of frostbite.' Harry sniggered. 'Would you believe I lost a finger and a toe – ?'

'What! That sounds serious.'

'No, I'm fine, I was well looked after.' He snorted. 'Great nurses.' He coughed.

Nyla went silent for a split second. 'I must tell you –'

'What?'

'They died –'

'Who did?'

'The policeman and Savina –'

'Zavos?'

'Yeah – they both died. It was in the papers, two or three weeks ago.'

Harry hid his excitement with a yawn. 'Ah.' He continued. 'So that's it then.'

'Yes, it is,' said Nyla. 'It's over.'

He lit a cigarette before speaking and took his time as he tried to hide the satisfaction in his voice. He blew smoke towards the camera. 'All the snow's gone and spring is just around the corner.'

'Yes, it's getting a bit warmer here now.' She looked directly at the camera. 'I wish you were still here,' she said pensively. 'We had such great fun and I loved working at the bar.'

Harry sighed. 'I know, love. But who knows what the future will bring, eh?'

Epilogue

The world media covered the story with the information uncovered by Harry and made public by Nichole. The huge child paedophile ring, linked to many of the prominent people who lived in Cyprus and other European countries, was followed by arrests and the eventual imprisonment of public figures from all walks of life.

Harry sat in his cottage and smiled to himself as he watched the news, and videos on YouTube, that exposed and unravelled the vile world of the paedophiles.

'Nice one, Nichole,' he said. 'This story will make your name for life.' He smiled to himself. 'Who knows you might end up working in London.'

He deleted the video links, sipped at his coffee and skyped Nyla.

'Hi, Dad, it's Thursday,' she said.

'Hi, love. I know.'

He lit a cigarette.

'I can see you now.'

'Good,' said Harry. He nodded and took a drag of his

cigarette. 'Someone wants to talk to you.' He paused. 'Before I introduce you … how about you come over and stay with me for a while?'

She shrieked her response. '*Fantastic.*'

'OK, we'll arrange it.' He stood up and continued. 'Here you go,' he said, as he left the room.

He walked into the kitchen and flicked on the radio. The song he heard seemed to be just for him. As Elton John sang, '*I'm still standing*' Harry smiled to himself. He talked to the radio. 'Yes, I am,' he said with the widest grin.

Nooda and Haya sat on the settee in front of the laptop and faced the camera.

They waved and shouted excitedly. 'Hello, Nyla.'

'Wow. How lovely to see you both,' screeched Nyla. 'What are you doing there with my dad?'

'It's a long story,' they said in unison.